Acknowledgements

Many thanks to Willie Pepper of Bradan Fanad Teo and Roy Redpath of Salmara, both of whom gave a great deal of technical advice about fish farming and checked the finished story for technical errors.

Song of the River

SOINBHE LALLY

BEACON BOOKS

POOLBEG

For Anna and Sheena

Published in 1995 by
Poolbeg Press Ltd,
Knocksedan House,
123 Baldoyle Industrial Estate,
Dublin 13, Ireland

Reprinted February 1997

A catalogue record for this book is available from the British Library.

ISBN 1 85371 457 7

Cover illustration by Rick Byrne
Cover design by Poolbeg Group Services Ltd
Set by Poolbeg Group Services Ltd in Joanna 12/13.5
Printed by The Guernsey Press Company Ltd,
Vale, Guernsey, Channel Islands.

Contents

Prologue   1

1   In a Cage   4
2   The Call of the River   13
3   Killing Day   18
4   Lost   26
5   On the Outside   30
6   A Monofilament Net   35
7   The Story of the King of the Fish   42
8   Attacked by Seals   54
9   The Story of the Tinker   63
10 A Baby Seal and An Otter   71
11 The River   81
12 Willie's Story   85
13 Death in the River   94
14 A Science Project   105
15 Searching   110
16 Fingal and the Gods   116
17 Found   121
18 Slurry   125
19 Spawning   129
20 The Song of the Sea   134

ABOUT THE AUTHOR

Soinbhe Lally was born in Enniskillen, County Fermanagh and was educated at Dominican Convent Portstewart, County Derry, and Queens University, Belfast, where she took an Arts Degree. She married and settled in County Donegal and has four children. Soinbhe Lally teaches in Ballyshannon Vocational School. She began writing short stories and satirical items in the *Fermanagh News* and has published stories in the *Irish Press New Writing* and various magazines including the prestigious US *Atlantic Monthly*. She is also a playwright and a winner of the Hennessy Award. Her novels for children include *A Hive for the Honey-Bee* and *The Hungry Wind*.

Prologue

High among wet peaty hills, the river began. It tumbled and churned under yellow froth, and lay in deep black pools. It grew and was joined by tributary streams. Then it ran deep and wide between steep clay riverbanks.

It meandered among rushy fields which flooded in winter. It became a lake, dotted with wooded islands. Then it narrowed and was a river once more, spanned by the bridges of a town. Below the town it widened into a lake which spread across a wide valley floor.

At last it came within sight of the sea. Once again it narrowed into a deep fast flowing river. It was captured by men and harnessed within the high walls of a dam, its immense power used to generate electricity. Below the dam it escaped again. It dashed between the concrete walls of a tail-race and under a grey stone bridge.

On a bright day in March when a blue sky and warm midday sun gave intimations of spring, a boy and girl stood on the bridge resting their elbows on the parapet. They both looked upstream towards the hydro-electric station. They wore identical brown school jumpers with gaudy yellow and red crests bearing the name of their school.

"Well?" demanded the girl.

"I don't know," the boy said reluctantly. His friends, seated on the parapet at the end of the bridge, hooted and whistled.

Ashling had been following Shawn round for most of lunch-time asking him to talk to her for a minute. He had ignored her for as long as he could but now she had him cornered. His friends were amused and shouted comments. They had succeeded in embarrassing him but he suspected they were envious too. Ashling was the prettiest girl in the class. What they didn't know was that she only wanted to talk about his science project.

"I told Mr Green I didn't want to do worms or liver fluke and he said I could do salmon with you," she persisted.

"You don't know anything about salmon."

"I could find out."

"How?"

He knew she came to school on a yellow school bus from fifteen miles inland. What would she know about salmon? His family had been salmon fishermen for generations. His great Uncle Willie was the best fisherman on the river estuary. Shawn could do a science project on salmon because he knew about salmon.

"I can read up on it," Ashling insisted, "I'll go and see them in the fish hatchery."

The fish hatchery? Now that was a good idea. Shawn hadn't thought of that. Maybe Ashling would be able to help after all. She could do lots of writing up too. Girls were good at that sort of stuff.

"All right," he agreed, "but stop following me around."

"Well, stand still the next time I want to talk to you," she retorted. She turned with a toss of her yellow hair and went off up the town.

"What did she want?" his friends asked eagerly when he sauntered back to them, trying hard to look casual.

"Not a lot," he said cryptically and ignored further questions. He heaved himself up on the parapet and looked down the river to the white bar of the rivermouth a mile or so below. Maybe this year Uncle Willie would let him fish with him.

The river shone in the bright light of midday. A few hundred yards downstream it frothed and foamed where it left the tailrace and entered a deep rocky basin. Beyond that, it meandered across a wide sandy estuary to where sea surf pounded on the river bar.

Its journey did not end there. The power of its current carried it far into the ocean, still flowing in its own freshwater stream between walls of brine. For twenty miles or more the river laid its own currents and eddies on the ocean, until salt water and fresh merged so completely that in the end, only a fish could tell the difference.

Then some deeply buried memory would revive and a silver salmon would remember his river, remember that it was time to return to the fresh water stream where he was spawned.

1

In a Cage

Fingal was sick. Waves of nausea swept over him. There was no escaping the filthy taste. He sank to the bottom of the cage, listing to one side. He wished he could die and float belly up at the surface till the gulls came screeching and squabbling, trying to penetrate the net which covered the fish cage. He tried not to feel so sorry for himself. He wouldn't really want to die, he argued with himself, not before he had gone outside the meshes of the cage and seen the vast ocean world beyond.

A large salmon swam down and joined him at the bottom of the cage. It was Gaffer. "What a waste of good fish pellets," he groaned, as the food pellets the men had brought drifted through the mesh floor. "I'll hate myself for not eating them, next time I feel hungry." Gaffer's appetite was famous. He was always hungry. Even on hot days in the summer, when the ocean was warm and nobody felt much like eating, he ate his own share and as much of everybody else's as one fish possibly could. "Feeling bad?" he asked sympathetically.

"Awful." Fingal listed a little more till he was almost on his side.

"Straighten yourself up," Gaffer urged. "Don't give in to it. The current should carry it away soon. I can feel a storm coming. That will clear the water."

With an effort Fingal held himself upright. "Pig slurry, that's what it is," he said.

"What?"

"I heard the men talking about it. They said a farmer put this filthy stuff into the bay. They called it pig slurry. That's why we're sick. We've been poisoned."

Gaffer listened in wonderment. He had often heard the men talking but understood very little of what they said. "I wonder what is a farmer," he pondered. "Is it a fish or a bird or one of those land creatures with many legs?"

"You mean a dog?" said Fingal. They had seen a dog once with men who came to look at the cage. "No, I don't think a dog would be a farmer. I mean, the dog made a lot of noise but it seemed harmless."

"A farmer is a man," said a voice.

"No, that can't be right. Men are good," Fingal answered absently. Then he started as he realised the voice was unfamiliar.

"You think men are good?" the voice asked. It was a sneering voice. Fingal looked around, puzzled. There was only Gaffer near to him. "Did you say something?" he asked.

"Me?"

"Was it you?" Fingal could see no one else.

"Down here, you fool," said the voice again.

Fingal peered through the floor of the cage. Below, he saw a large silver sea trout, weighty and broad with years. He had seen sea trout before. They often came at feeding time to snatch any fishmeal pellets that had not been eaten by the salmon.

"Did you say something?" Fingal asked.

"I asked you if you really believe that men are good?"

"Of course they are," Gaffer interrupted. "They feed us. They bring us our food, even in stormy weather. You see how they bring us fishmeal pellets three times a day."

"Oh you idiot," sneered the trout. "Don't you know why they feed you?"

"Why?" Fingal asked uneasily. He was afraid that the answer would be something he would prefer not to hear.

The trout looked immensely old and knowledgeable. Inside the cage the salmon were all the same age. They had been together since they were young salmon eggs in the nursery tanks in the fish hatchery.

The men had always been there. The men were the first thing that Fingal remembered. Men were creatures of the world beyond the water's surface. He had been only an egg, an embryo with two wide astonished eyes looking through the membrane of his egg sac, when he first noticed a man gazing into their nursery tank.

"Eight degrees," said the man, checking an instrument. It was much later that Fingal learned the name of the instrument, a thermometer. "Eight degrees." Those were the first words he had heard from the humankind who cared for them. It was much later still before he understood them. "Eight degrees. Thirty-one days. Eyed Ova," said the man, causing a slight disturbance in the water which flowed through the long narrow nursery tank, as he removed the thermometer.

The man came every day. At five hundred and ten degree days, Fingal hatched from his egg sac and found himself just one of thousands of small, squirming, transparent alevins hardly half an inch long. "What are we?" Fingal asked wriggling among them, snuggling into the shadow of a green plastic grid, away from the light and they all echoed his question, asking "What are we? What are we?" but none of them could offer an answer.

For a month he fed on his egg sac. Then suddenly it was all gone. He grew hungry. "I'm hungry," he realised, and irritably flicked his minute body. He left the shelter of the green plastic and swam high in the water. There, he found that all the others had swum up already. "Swimming up stage," said the man with the thermometer and sprinkled a fine brown dust into the water. It floated briefly on the surface and then began to sink. Fingal was irked at the intrusion of the floating specks into his water. He snapped at a grain of the dust which floated impertinently in front of him. The man tossed more brown dust on the surface. The tiny fish were annoyed. They snapped angrily. Then Fingal realised what it was. "It's food!" he exclaimed, "it's for eating!"

"Food! It's food," chorused all the tiny fish and they started feeding.

"First feeding fry," noted the man with satisfaction and he withdrew the thermometer from the tank.

"Fry?" wondered Fingal. He looked at himself and then at the others. They had changed. Their bodies were no longer transparent. They were growing scales. Fry, of course! "We're fry," he exclaimed delightedly and the others echoed, "We're fry! We're fry!"

They were fished out of their nursery tank and put into an enormous blue tank where incredibly bright daylight entered through a single open panel in its roof. The man no longer fed them. An automatic feeder dropped food on the surface at regular intervals. They continued to grow. Dark shadows, like the shadows of ripples on the tank floor, appeared on their bodies. "Salmon parr," observed the man, making a note in his records.

"Salmon parr! That's what we are now," exclaimed Fingal.

"Salmon parr?" said the others incredulously. "But we're fry."

"The man called us salmon parr," said Fingal and the little fish chattered excitedly about their transformation.

They grew larger still. The hours of daylight lengthened and when the sun shone into their tank at midday, Fingal noticed how they had grown long, almost six inches long. The ripple shadows that marked their bodies a few months earlier had disappeared and their scales had grown silver. "What are we now?" he wondered and felt a vague urge to leave the wide blue tank and go – where did he want to go?

They heard from the man where they would go. "Sixty thousand salmon smolt will go to the sea, this week," he said to the men who came to help with netting the young smolt in readiness for their journey. It was a moist morning in April, a morning when the river water which flowed through the tank had lost its winter chill and made the young fish restless, full of unnameable urges.

"The sea, that's it, we're salmon smolt and it is time to go to the sea," said Fingal and the others agreed excitedly.

"Yes, we must leave this tank and find the sea," they said enthusiastically but nobody knew exactly how it could be done.

Now, more than a year later, Fingal still remembered how it was done although the recollection was so incredible that he sometimes thought he must have dreamed it. The men took them from the big blue tanks and put them, four thousand at a time, into small metal tanks. Then they closed a lid over them. A huge roaring flying machine hoisted the tanks in the air and flew through the sky. Fingal had often seen the sky through the open panel in the tank where they had lived for so long. Now, he glimpsed the sky briefly when the suspended tank swayed to and fro, loosening the lid and spilling water and even a couple of smolt into the empty air. He glimpsed a vast expanse of moving green surface far below and was sick with fear. Then they were lowered with a horrible sinking sensation to the ocean surface. The lid of the transport tank was opened. Fingal could see the swinging cable from which they were suspended and above it, through the heaving surface of the tank water, the huge rotating blades of the monstrous machine. It hovered above, making an appalling sound. The helicopter, he heard the men call it.

Then, magically, they were dropped into the ocean, a vast green ocean. Frantic with joy they rushed about, tasting salt water for the first time. This, they knew, was what they had been born for. It was for this briny deep that they had turned silver. Now they were young salmon, swimming, at last, in the ocean.

They rushed to explore the vast empty spaces of the sea but instead, collided with the mesh walls that surrounded them. Again and again they rushed at them. They beat their bodies against them till they ached all over but to no avail. They realised that the vast ocean was not for them. They were in a cage.

At first it was not so bad. It was a very large cage, thirty metres across and sixty metres deep. They were young and did not take up much space. However that was a long time ago. At least it seemed a long time. They were now fully grown. Gaffer, the biggest of them, was more than half as long as a man.

It was crowded in the cage. Too crowded. Some days the salmon became angry and flung themselves in fury against the mesh walls. There was no way out. The only way out was to die, and float belly up on the surface. Then the men would take you away. Fingal had seen fish die and float upside down at the surface till the men removed them from the cage.

"You farm salmon are idiots. Utter idiots," sneered the old trout. "You know nothing, do you? You don't know that men are cunning, and prey on us fish?"

"No they're not," Gaffer retorted indignantly. "They feed us. They care for us. The men are kind."

"Haven't you ever seen a killing day?" asked the old trout.

"What's a killing day?" asked Fingal. He had straightened up now but he didn't really feel any better. The conversation with the sea trout was making him uneasy and fearful. Perhaps the old trout did know things they did not know. He was free to roam the ocean and would see and hear things that Fingal and the salmon in the cage could never know about.

"Don't you know about killing day?" the trout went on. "Well, I don't know if I should tell you about it at all. You won't much like hearing it."

"Please do tell us," Fingal asked. He wanted to know and at the same time dreaded knowing.

"Very well."

"I think you're just making things up," Gaffer argued. He didn't like this trout. He didn't like the way he sneered and made Fingal afraid. Gaffer wasn't afraid of anything. He knew he was the biggest, strongest salmon in the cage, perhaps in the whole ocean. He didn't have to fear anything a trout could tell him.

"Please don't interrupt," said the trout. "If you won't listen with manners, I can go away. That's more than you can do."

"Oh no, please don't go. Tell us about killing day," Fingal pleaded, but he already had his suspicions. He had sensed the frantic motion of fish in distress, not far away, at certain times when the men came by with their barges but always passed the cage without stopping. On those days there was a smell of death on the tidal currents. He had always known the smell of death. Yet it happened with such regularity that it seemed as natural as the storms and the calms and the seaweed that grew and was torn from the seabed and floated in great clumps at the surface.

"Killing day is the day on which the men take the salmon from their cages and kill them. You've felt it, haven't you? You must have smelled death on the tidal current. Every creature in the sea can smell death when it happens nearby." The old trout leered delightedly. "Well, haven't you?"

"I don't believe you." It was Gaffer who spoke. "The men have never killed any of us."

"You think yours is the only cage?"

"Are . . . there others?" Fingal asked hesitantly.

"Lots. There are lots of cages. Some with salmon bigger and older than you . . . "

"Bigger than me?" said Gaffer incredulously.

"Yes, of course, bigger than you," said the trout. "And just as stupid."

"Tell us about the other cages," Fingal asked.

"As I was saying," the trout went on, "some of the fish are bigger than you and some are just smolts,

11

newly arrived from the hatchery on the river. They flew in a whole lot of tanks full of them just last week. What a laugh that was, when they tried to swim for the open sea. It always gives us trout a laugh to see how you salmon swim into the walls of your cages. You fools."

"But what is killing day? What does it mean?" Fingal had to know.

"It's the day that you salmon are big enough and fat enough for the men to eat. They come and pump you out of the cages into a big tank. Then you die. Oh yes, I've seen it. I'm an old fish. I've seen a lot of things in my time. Nasty things. I nearly got caught myself once, in a fisherman's bag net, but that's another story. As I was saying, you salmon are sucked up into that big tank and then they kill you one by one . . . "

"Stop it," shouted Gaffer, beating his tail furiously against the wall of the cage. "I don't believe you. Stop it, you liar!"

"Well," the trout bristled indignantly, "if you don't want to know, that's your problem. I'm not staying here to be insulted." With a swish of his tail he darted away.

"No, no, please come back," Fingal called. He desperately needed to know more. "Do come back. Gaffer didn't mean it."

It was no use. The old trout was gone. Now they would never know. At least, not until it happened.

2

The Call of the River

Gaffer was right about the weather. The storm struck a few hours later and swept the ocean clean of the foul taste and smell. Fingal felt a great deal better when the men came with the evening feed, their boat tossing crazily on the waves. Anybody could see that the sea was not the natural element of men. He could see their bright yellow waterproofs as they moved carefully on the platform above the cage and completed their task as quickly as possible so that they could return safely to the land.

Fingal was very hungry. He leaped and thrashed among the other fish, snatching his share of food pellets till he was comfortably full. He felt grateful to the men. When he thought again about the old trout he decided that he was simply jealous because he could not come into the cage and be fed, like the salmon. The only pellets he got were the few that were overlooked by the hungry salmon and drifted down through the bottom of the cage. And even there he had to compete with other trout and sea creatures who gathered to seize upon any tasty morsel that dropped from the salmon cage. The men were kind and the things the trout said about them couldn't possibly be true.

By the following morning the storm had passed.

13

Huge drifts of tangled seaweed drifted by. The sea tasted fresh and tangy and the salmon cavorted and played, full of the high spirits that always infected them after a storm. Fingal and Gaffer noticed the big old trout who had spoken to them the previous day, nosing ineffectually about the underside of the cage, and they jeered at him.

"Scram, old fellow," said Gaffer, making a playful charge in his direction but stopping short to avoid colliding with the mesh floor of the cage.

"No leftovers today, I'm afraid," said Fingal with mock sympathy. "We seem to have eaten everything. But do hang around for lunch. We've had so much for breakfast, we mightn't be able to eat everything."

The old trout glowered silently at them and then swam away. Fingal and Gaffer hooted after him.

"That's not very kind, is it, fish?" said a gentle voice. "I'm surprised at you, Fingal. And you, Gaffer. Teasing a poor, hungry old trout."

Fingal and Gaffer recoiled in embarrassment. It was Silverfin who spoke. She was a shining, silver hen salmon, prettier, Fingal thought, than any other hen salmon in the cage, with a kind, gentle expression. Fingal felt suddenly ashamed of his behaviour.

"He said nasty things about the men," he explained lamely.

"I think sea trout must be great liars," Gaffer added.

"Well I think the two of you should be ashamed of yourselves," said Silverfin sternly. "You shouldn't tease the wild fish. Just because they are less fortunate than us is no reason to despise them."

"I'm sorry," said Fingal, "I won't do it again." He liked Silverfin far too much to quarrel with her.

"And you, Gaffer?"

"All right, I'll leave him alone, unless he comes here telling more lies."

They played at the surface for hours that evening. The water turned gold, then deep red and finally darkness fell. It was time to sleep but Fingal felt oddly restless.

"Do you feel it?" he asked Gaffer.

"Feel what?"

"That . . . I don't know what it is. It's as if someone was calling me."

"You mean, you're hearing things?"

"No, I don't hear it, but I feel it. Something is drawing me. I don't know what it is. Don't you feel it, Gaffer?"

"No I don't. Go to sleep, you crazy fish."

Was he crazy, Fingal wondered. Perhaps he was, he mused sleepily. In which case, next morning, all the other fish in the cage were crazy too.

Gaffer butted him awake early. "I feel it, I hear it," he exclaimed. "I know now what you mean."

"What do you mean by wakening me up so early," Fingal grumbled. "You're disturbing everybody."

However, as he shook himself awake, he realised that everybody else was already awake. There was unusual agitation in the cage. Fish were swimming round and round, searching fruitlessly for an opening in the walls of the cage. Fingal felt an overwhelming sense of longing. He must get out. He must go. Something was calling him.

"What is it?" Gaffer asked in bewilderment. "What is this feeling? It's unbearable." He rushed to the mesh wall and thrashed himself against it again and again.

"Stop it, that's no use. You can't get out that way," Fingal said. Gaffer was injuring himself. Shreds of damaged skin hung from his tail. There was a sudden commotion among the fish on the other side of the cage. Fingal and Gaffer rushed over to see if they had found an exit but all that was there was a group of wild salmon who had paused outside the cage, astonished to see so many of their own kind together in one place.

"What are you doing in there?" a large hen salmon asked curiously, peering through the meshes at the thousands of fish inside. "Aren't you going to the river?"

"What's the river?" someone asked.

"What's the river?" echoed the hen salmon in astonishment. "What kind of salmon are you? Did you not come from the river?"

The farm salmon looked at each other, bewildered. They remembered the blue tank. But was that the river? Nobody knew for sure. "I think we flew here," Fingal said dubiously.

The hen salmon turned to Gaffer. "Is he crazy?" she asked.

"Sometimes," Gaffer said because he remembered calling Fingal a crazy fish the previous night.

"But how can you not know about the river? Don't you feel it? Can't you feel it calling you? Don't you hear the song of the river?"

"The song of the river," the caged fish echoed, "of course, that's what it is, the call of the river." Suddenly they knew the meaning of the terrible longing which possessed them. They trembled all over with excitement. It was the song of the river. Their river wanted them. The river from which they came when they were young smolts was calling for them to come back again.

"Where is the river?" Fingal asked. He knew he could never go. Knowing would never satisfy his longing for it, but still, he needed to know.

"Which is your river?" asked the wild salmon.

"I don't know," Fingal replied miserably. He hadn't realised that there was more than one river. "How many rivers are there?"

"Oh, hundreds."

"And how do you find your own river?"

"We swim south, following the coast till we come to it. When we find it we know."

The large hen salmon turned away and joined the group of wild salmon. "We must go now," she said, turning to leave, "our river is calling us."

Yes, our river is calling, thought every salmon in the cage and they looked, with immense yearning, towards the south, in the direction in which the wild salmon had swum away.

3

Killing Day

They continued to hear the song of the river intermittently over the days and weeks which followed. Sometimes they could forget it entirely and then, at other times, they were possessed by an inexpressible longing for that place which none of them could clearly remember.

"I remember the big round tank. It was blue like the sky," Fingal said reminiscently.

"I remember the water," said Silverfin. "That is, I don't remember what it was like but I remember that when we came here the water tasted quite differently. Don't you remember how exciting that was?"

"Did we eat pellets in the fish tanks?" Gaffer asked.

"Trust Gaffer to think of food," Bubble giggled. She was a giddy hen salmon, not nearly so pretty as Silverfin but agile and swift and full of mischief and fun. Everyone could see she liked Gaffer, except Gaffer himself who never seemed to notice.

"Well, I can't remember anything about the tanks. I just thought some of you would know. I don't see what's so funny," he said as they all laughed at him.

Bubble somersaulted in delight. "You're so funny," she said, "you funny big fish."

They were so absorbed in their conversation that they did not notice death draw close to them. Nor did they notice how appallingly different it was this time.

Silverfin was the first to remark on the peculiar behaviour of the wild fish. A shoal of mackerel had rushed frantically by. That was not so odd. Mackerel were always in a great hurry. But then, a moment later, a dozen awkward fat ballan wrasse blundered past. Some of them collided with the mesh side of the cage in their haste.

"Are you all right?" Silverfin asked solicitously.

"Help! Save us!" cried the wrasse in unison and then they dashed away without explaining what was wrong.

"Come back," Bubble shouted after them. "What's the matter with you?"

She fell suddenly silent. All of them sensed that death was somewhere close by. It was puzzling. They were conscious that it was not the usual weekly routine of death. The men had not passed in their barges. This was something different. Today was not killing day.

"Feeling scared, I'll bet," said a sneering voice below them. Fingal and Gaffer recognised the voice of the trout.

"What do you want?" said Gaffer menacingly.

"It's not what I want that matters just now, is it?" the trout replied.

"I'm afraid I don't understand," said Silverfin politely. "Perhaps you can tell us what is happening out on your side of the cage?"

"Oh, nothing very much," said the trout nonchalantly. "Just a killer whale paying a courtesy visit to the bay."

"A whale?" Bubble asked interestedly. "Is that a fish?"

"Well, a whale looks quite like a fish and he swims like a fish but I've been told on very good authority that he's not really a fish. You see, he has no gills," said the trout, delighted to show off his knowledge of the subject.

19

"What does a whale have to do with us?" demanded Gaffer. He was determined not to trust the old trout who had told them such ridiculous lies.

"A whale has quite a large appetite," said the trout.

"Not as big as Gaffer's, I'll bet," interrupted Bubble with a giggle.

"Even bigger than Gaffer's, I should think," said the trout. "He eats huge quantities of fish. And there's nothing he likes better for a snack than a nice, plump, well fed salmon."

"But that's impossible," said Fingal. "We're the biggest fish in the sea. None of you wild fish is big enough to eat one of us."

"I told you, a killer whale isn't really a fish. He's a monster and he's huge. A thousand times bigger than any salmon."

"Is he as big as the men's boat?" ventured Silverfin.

"Bigger."

"As big as the barge?"

"Much, much bigger."

Silverfin shuddered.

"Don't you believe a word he says," said Fingal indignantly. He was furious with the trout for frightening Silverfin. He turned to the trout. "If a killer whale is such a fearsome monster, why are you still here instead of rushing away to hide yourself like the other wild fish?"

"You're a silly salmon, aren't you," retorted the trout. "Can't you feel it? The whale has gone away now. For a little while at least."

The trout was right. The sense of the closeness of death had faded while they spoke. Fingal had been too irritated to notice. The group of ballan wrasse which they had seen fleeing in panic a few minutes earlier passed by the cage again, heading back to their feeding grounds, as if nothing had happened to frighten them.

"Of course, a killer whale will be the least of your problems this week, I should think," sneered the trout.

"Oh yes?" retorted Gaffer, "there's something else you want to try to scare us with, is there?"

"Would I dream of doing such a thing? Of course, there is one little matter which might interest you."

"And what might that be?" Gaffer asked, trying to sound as sarcastic as the trout.

"Nothing really. I suppose it's not important at all. It's just that they emptied cage number 5 on the last killing day. But I don't suppose you would be interested in knowing that, would you?"

"Is there any reason why we should?"

"Not really, except that you may not have noticed that yours is cage number 5." The trout flicked his tail and with a hoot of laughter darted away.

Bubble was first to break the silence when he had gone. "What did he mean? What is killing day?"

"It's just nonsense. That trout is a really mean fish. He makes up things to try to scare us," Fingal reassured her but he had an uncomfortable feeling that the trout might know what he was talking about.

"Well," said Silverfin, "I can understand why you and Gaffer were so rude to him. He really is a nasty trout, isn't he?"

Fingal agreed but inwardly he wondered if he should not believe the trout. Suppose he had told the truth. That would mean that it would be the turn of their cage on the next killing day. They would all be killed, one by one. It wasn't possible. No, it was unthinkable. Anyway, who would believe a trout who talked such nonsense about a creature which was a fish and not a fish, and which was bigger than a barge. Killer whale indeed! It was too incredible.

Next morning there was no breakfast feed of fish pellets. The salmon circled hopefully, listening for the sound of the men's boat engine. An hour passed. Then in the distance they heard the dull reverberation of an engine pulse through the water. The men were coming at last. Eagerly, they rushed to the surface and waited.

However, the men were not in their usual boat. They had come on the biggest of the barges and there were many men, not just the two whom they saw every day. Gaffer and Fingal swam nervously to the bottom of the cage. Everything was wrong. The routine was different. The men hadn't brought food. They were working and shouting at the surface and yet there was no sight of food pellets in the water. They hadn't come to feed the salmon.

Gaffer voiced their suspicions. "Do you think it's our turn?"

"You mean, killing day?" Fingal shuddered.

"Hey, you guys, why are you skulking down here?" Bubble swam down to them. "You'll miss out on feeding. Everybody's at the surface." She turned to swim away again.

"No, stay down here," Gaffer called to her. "It might be safer."

She turned back to them. "Safer? Have you been listening to that old trout again?"

"Something's wrong," said Fingal urgently. "This isn't a regular feeding. Everything's different. This is killing day."

"What do you mean?" Bubble tried not to be afraid but her fins quivered a little.

"The trout told us. On killing day they pump us out of the cage, into a big tank and then they kill us."

"But the men wouldn't do a thing like that, would they?"

As if in reply to her question, an enormous pipe was lowered into the water above them. They cowered against the floor of the cage, terrified of the monstrous thing.

"Isn't it exciting!" exclaimed Silverfin, dashing down to join them. "What do you think they can be doing? Perhaps they are taking us back to the river. Do come and see. What are you hiding down here for?"

"It's killing day," said Bubble, "they're going to kill us."

"That's not a nice thing to say," Silverfin reproved her. "The men would never do anything to hurt us."

"Stay with us here," urged Fingal. "I don't know if we can escape that thing but I think we'll have a better chance if we stay as far from it as we can."

As he spoke they heard the roar of a motor at the surface and a fierce suction of water passed through the cage. The pipe was lowered even further into the cage. "Swim against it, swim for your lives," called Gaffer. They fought it furiously, swimming with all their strength away from sucking power of the pipe.

"I can't," said Silverfin, swimming as hard as she could but still being drawn upwards. "I can't. Please, Fingal, don't leave me. Don't let me go in there alone."

"Stay close to me," Fingal urged, "Don't give up."

"I can't. It's too strong," she gasped, drawn backwards and stifled by the rush of water against her gills. She was drawn further and further, towards the mouth of the pump. Other fish were submitting passively to the suction, unaware of any danger.

"Fingal, please, help me," Silverfin cried.

Fingal hesitated. Was there any point in fighting against it? Could he let Silverfin go in there without him? He saw her disappear into the pipe and turned to follow.

"Don't go," Gaffer called after him but Fingal ignored his warning. The pipe loomed nearer and nearer. Salmon crowded around it. Death was in the pipe. Fingal felt death all around him in the water. He was caught in the stream of water created by the suction of the pipe. There was no turning back now. The suction was too powerful. He was almost in the mouth of the pipe when the suction stopped abruptly. At the same instant he realised that another sort of death had struck the cage, struck with shocking, unforeseeable violence. Something far greater, far vaster and far more fearsome than the pump had entered the cage.

The mesh walls were violently sundered. The suction pipe was tossed aside. Fingal had a glimpse of huge snapping jaws. There was blood in the water, the blood of salmon. A vast, monstrous thing flung itself about, smashing the cage. It snatched and gobbled. For a brief instant Fingal found himself close to an incredibly enormous eye. He knew now that the trout had spoken the truth. This was a killer whale, far bigger than any boat or barge.

He recoiled in a frenzy of terror, rushing away from the fearsome thing. It made a violent heave and suddenly it was right before him again. Fingal turned frantically away. The water thrashed and churned. He was whirled and tossed about. He no longer knew which way was up and which was down. Desperately, he lashed with his powerful tail, driving blindly through the turbulence around him.

On and on he swam, in blind panic, crashing into other salmon as panic-stricken as himself. He swerved wildly away from them and away from the black, monstrous killer whale. At last he swam clear of the turbulence and found himself in open sea, no longer surrounded by walls of mesh. Desperately he swam on and on till he was too tired to swim any more. Then he sank exhausted to the ocean floor and hid in the shelter of seaweed, dimly aware that for the first time in his entire life he was alone, utterly alone.

4

Lost

He lay in the sheltering seaweed all night long. He remained motionless, too tired and too frightened to move. Next day, small ballan wrasse emerged timidly from their niches in a nearby rock and peered at him curiously. Reassured when he did not move, they approached closer and nosed about him.

"You're a stranger here, aren't you?" inquired one of them, curiously.

"Yes," Fingal agreed. Wrasse were silly, inquisitive creatures but just now he was glad of their company. He was desperately lonely. He wondered what had become of his friends. Had they been killed by the whale? Or had they suffered Silverfin's fate in the men's killing tank? Was he the only survivor or were there others? Even if any of the others had escaped, how would he ever find them? The ocean was impossibly vast. It was unlikely that he would see any of them ever again.

"Travelling to your river, are you?" enquired an old thick scaled wrasse whose body was brown with age.

"No, I'm lost," said Fingal miserably.

"Lost?" echoed the wrasse crowding around curiously. They had never seen a lost salmon before.

"Where have you come from?" asked the old wrasse, "if you can tell us, we might be able to show you the way. We know this rocky part of the shore better than anybody."

"I've come from a cage at the salmon farm," said Fingal. "It was attacked by a killer whale."

"Killer whale!" shrieked the smaller wrasse, rushing in terror to the shelter of their niches in the rock. Then realising that their fright was unfounded they came out again, one by one, looking with astonishment and admiration at Fingal.

"How did you get away?" asked the old wrasse with new respect in his voice.

"The whale smashed the cage and I just swam and swam and swam...till I was here," said Fingal. "And now I'm lost. I don't know where I am and I don't know where to go. I don't know how to survive. I've never been a wild fish. The men always took care of me."

"The men took care of you?" said the old wrasse incredulously. "I've never heard of such a thing. I thought men only killed fish."

"Yes, they did do that too," agreed Fingal. "They were just starting to kill us when the whale came."

"You mean, you escaped from the men as well as the whale?" said the old wrasse, enormously impressed. "You're a cunning one, aren't you?"

"I was just lucky," said Fingal modestly.

"Yes, you were lucky too. I've tangled with men, myself. It takes luck as well as cunning to get away from them. Look at this." The old wrasse turned sideways to show Fingal a rusty stump of a hook embedded in the corner of his mouth. "I made the mistake of snatching a nice fat lugworm without looking to see why it was floating so enticingly in front of me. Only that I had the presence of mind to dive

27

and wrap the fisherman's line round a strong clump of seaweed, I would have been a dead fish that time. Look, there's the hook still in my mouth, do you see it?"

"You mean, a man did that to you?" said Fingal, shocked. "But why?"

"I suppose he wanted a nice fat wrasse for his dinner," said the old fish cheerfully. "I learned my lesson. I'm a very old fish now, thanks to that lesson. And I've had many a delicious snack from a fisherman's hook since then but I've never been so foolish as to let any of them catch me."

"He's the cunningest fish in the whole sea," lisped one very small wrasse with admiration. "He can nibble every bit of bait off a hook and the fisherman doesn't notice till it's all gone."

"Well, young salmon, I'm sure you don't want to listen to the entire life history of an old fish like me. I suppose you're anxious to get back to where you came from."

"Yes please, I'd be grateful if you'd show me the way."

"We'll be glad to. But first we have to feed. Would you like to join us?" invited the old wrasse.

Fingal realised he hadn't eaten for more than a day. He gladly followed the wrasse inshore. They stopped at a bed of small seed mussels quite near to where waves broke against the shore. Fingal was excited and curious. He had never seen the shore before. It was rugged and high, much higher than the highest waves. The wrasse were amused at his astonishment.

"We can only eat here at high tide," the old wrasse explained, "when the seed mussel bed is covered with water. At low tide this is dry land."

"Land? What is land?" asked Fingal.

"It's where the men live. You see how they move about on two tails. That's because they live on land."

"Those are not tails, they're legs," said Fingal. He knew a great deal more about men than the wrasse did, from his daily contact with them all his life.

"Legs?" said the wrasse contemptuously. "Yes, tail is too good a word for men. Legs. Humph. I must remember that."

"Let's eat," exclaimed one of the small wrasse impatiently and he darted down to the sea bottom.

"Yes, let's eat," agreed the old wrasse and he swam down with stately dignity to the mussel-covered rock.

Fingal followed him and watched in amazement as the ballan wrasse used their strong white teeth to rip the mussels from the rock and grind them up.

"Aren't you having any?" the old wrasse asked when he noticed Fingal had not started eating. "Here, try this," he said, nosing a clump of mussels towards Fingal. Fingal attempted to eat some of it but the shells were hard and sharp and hurt his mouth.

"I'm afraid I'm not very hungry," he said politely and then he waited till the wrasse had finished feeding and were ready to lead him to the cage. He felt a little frightened at the thought of going back to the cage. What if the killer whale were still there, or if the men were still trying to pump fish into their tank? However, it was his only hope of finding other salmon. Some of them must have survived. He had to believe that or he would surely die of loneliness.

5

On the Outside

The cage was deserted. One side of it was smashed and torn wide open.

"Gaffer," Fingal called. "Gaffer," he heard echo back from the empty distance. All of the salmon were gone without trace. The torn meshes suspended in the water and the platform, listing at a precarious tilt, were the only signs that the cage full of salmon had once been there.

"Are you sure this is the right cage?" asked the old ballan wrasse. "There are other cages. Would you like us to show them to you?"

"Are there salmon in them?" Fingal asked.

"Lots of salmon, just like you," chorused the smaller wrasse and they dashed off, eager to show the way.

The next cage was not very far away. Fingal was surprised that so many salmon could have been so close without his realising it before. It was an enormous relief to see fish of his own kind. He dashed to the mesh wall of the cage and called to the salmon inside. "Hey, you in there," he shouted, "have you seen any salmon pass this way?"

Several salmon answered together. "Are you from the broken cage? Where are you going? Did you see the whale? Was it terrible?"

"Quiet!" shouted one larger fish. "He can't answer all

of you at once. Let him get a word in edgeways." He turned to Fingal and explained, "Several fish from the broken cage passed this way yesterday. They told us about the whale."

"Do you know which way they went?" asked Fingal.

"That way."

"This way?"

"No, they went north."

"I saw them go south."

The salmon argued volubly. "I'm afraid we didn't ask them which way they were going," said the big salmon. "I don't think they knew themselves. They just wanted to get as far from that killer whale as they could. I'm sorry we can't give you more information."

"What is it like to be outside the cage?" asked one pretty, silver finned salmon curiously.

She reminded Fingal a little of Silverfin. He remembered that Silverfin had gone into the men's killing tank and must be dead by now. It was a painful thought which made him ache with loneliness. "It's very lonely," he said.

"But we're his friends," said the very small wrasse, mustering enough courage to speak to the salmon which were many times bigger than himself. He darted away shyly and hid behind the big old wrasse.

"We had better be off," said the old wrasse. "We ballan wrasse don't like to spend much time in the open sea, we'll head back to our own rocks now. Don't worry," he said kindly to Fingal, "you'll be all right with your new friends. I'm sure they'll take care of you." He turned to the small wrasse and called them, "Come along, you lot, it's time to go home." Together they swam away.

Fingal circled the cage over and over but it was just

like his own cage, there was no way in or out, unless you could do like a whale and smash your way in. His new salmon friends circled too, on the inside of the mesh.

"I can't think why you want in," said the big salmon who seemed to be the leader, just as Gaffer had been, in Fingal's cage. "I've been trying all my life to get out."

"Yes, but it's so lonely out here. And scary. I wouldn't mind being outside if I was with the others. We did want out. We often tried to get out."

He tried to think about that, about how much they had wanted out. He reminded himself that they would have been pumped into the men's tank for killing, if the whale had not come. Silverfin had gone into the big pipe and the men had killed her. He wondered if his new salmon friends knew about killing day. It would be better for them if they didn't know. He decided not to tell them that part of the story.

"The men are coming now," said the pretty salmon with silver fins. "It's feeding time."

Fingal realised suddenly how hungry he was. He had not eaten for two days. He swam eagerly to the surface and waited for the men to arrive. It was not till they had emptied the fishmeal pellets into the cage that he realised they were not for him. He was on the outside, like the wild fish. He would have to scavenge at the bottom of the cage like them. He swam down hopefully, ravenous now that he could see and smell the fishmeal pellets. It seemed an age till he saw a single pellet float through the mesh floor of the cage. Eagerly he rushed to snatch it. Something darted past him and he found himself snapping at empty water.

"Delicious," said a voice. "Absolutely delicious. I do

recommend these fish meal pellets. They make a splendid appetiser."

"You!" exploded Fingal in rage, "that was my pellet."

"I'm afraid it's every fish for himself down here," retorted the trout which had snatched the pellet. "The best fish wins. You just weren't quick enough."

Fingal recognised the old trout who had scavenged under their cage and who had told them about killing day. Of course, he would have had to move on and scavenge under another cage, now that Fingal's cage was destroyed. And he had snatched the only food pellet that had drifted down so far that meal time. Fingal was speechless with indignation.

"Well, you don't have much to say for yourself, now that you're a wild salmon, eh?" sneered the trout. "You'll find things very different here on the outside. Out here, the game is survival. But of course, you've already learned a little about that. If you hadn't, you would have made a nice snack for that killer whale yesterday, wouldn't you?"

Fingal didn't reply. He knew the trout was speaking the truth. He had always spoken the truth but Fingal had never wanted to believe him. He turned away.

"Hang around," the trout jeered after him, "maybe the salmon won't be so hungry at their next meal. Maybe you'll be a little quicker to snatch the next leftover."

Fingal remembered with shame how he and Gaffer had teased the trout and how Silverfin had scolded them for it. He turned back. "I'm sorry I teased you when I was in the cage. It was just, I didn't want to believe the things you told us. I wanted to think you were bad. I'm sorry. I understand now what it's like to have to find your own food. I didn't understand then."

"That's all right," said the trout magnanimously, "we all live and learn. By the way, if you're looking for your friends, they've gone to the river."

The river! Of course. Fingal could have laughed for joy. Why hadn't he thought of it before? How could he have forgotten about the river? Suddenly, the song of the river was all about him, on every side. "Do you hear it?" he cried out delightedly. "It's the song of the river."

"The song of the river," echoed the salmon inside the cage, "is that what it is? This terrible longing is for the river?"

"Yes indeed," said the trout, "the song of the river, the sweetest song an old trout can ever hear."

"You mean, you can hear it too?" said Fingal, astonished. "But you're a trout."

"Do you think salmon are the only fish to hear the call of the river? Believe me, young salmon, I have followed the call of the river more times than you know how to count."

"You know the way to the river?"

"I should think so."

Fingal forgot that he had been hungry. Food didn't matter any more. All that mattered was the call of the river. "Will you show me the way?"

"There are many rivers. I'm going to find my own river. You're welcome to come along if you think that's where you're going."

"When do you leave?" Fingal asked with growing excitement.

The old trout flicked his tail and turned towards the south. He looked back at Fingal. "Right now," he said and swam quickly away.

"Wait for me," called Fingal, hurrying after him.

6

A Monofilament Net

They swam for hours. The water above them turned gold, then red, then finally black and sparkling under the pale moon which wavered unsteadily among the ripples at the surface. The trout suddenly swerved from his southerly course and swam inshore. Fingal tasted fresh river water. He remembered at once that the water in the hatchery tanks had tasted fresh, without the salt tang of the sea. He was amazed that he could ever have forgotten. "Is it the river?" he asked excitedly.

"It's a river," replied the trout, "but I can't tell yet if it's my river. I must swim closer to taste it. Every trout knows the taste of his own river." He swam more slowly. Fingal dashed eagerly ahead. "Careful," warned the trout, "there's no hurry. We must go carefully now."

"Carefully? What are you afraid of?" Fingal was impatient to find the river.

"Stop, don't move," warned the trout.

"What's the matter?"

"It's a net."

"Where? I don't see anything." Fingal peered through the darkness. At first he could see nothing. Then, close to him, he saw a dead fish suspended in midwater. Further down, suspended in the same peculiar way, a

35

pollack gasped feebly, his gills caught in some invisible trap. The dead fish seemed to move. Fingal realised that the motion was the movement of several small crabs which were feasting on the corpse. He shuddered and backed away.

"It's a driftnet," the trout explained. "The men put them near rivers so that we will be caught in them. Sometimes they're easy to see but this is one of the invisible nets which they sometimes use. Monofilament nets, they call them. If there hadn't been other fish in it we wouldn't have known it was there."

"How will we reach the river now?"

"We must go round the net. But we'll wait till morning. We'll see more clearly by day."

They swam inshore to a warm shingle beach and slept there, resting on the coloured pebbles, rocked by small waves which rolled rhythmically above them.

In the morning, splintered sunlight shone through the water and when they approached the net again, they could occasionally glimpse its monofilament meshes undulating in the ebb and flow of the current. They swam along its length, moving cautiously. There were many fish trapped in it, some drowned after their night-long struggle and some, more recently caught, still struggling for freedom and survival.

At the bottom of the net, where a rope weighted with lead held it in place on the sea bed, were a dogfish and several ballan wrasse. Fingal remembered the wrasse who had helped him the previous day and was glad that they were far away from this net. He swam past an enormous mullet, also snared in the mesh, the nylon threads cutting into its powerful body. Then, almost at the end of the net, he saw a group of four salmon approach.

"Stop," he warned them but they were too far off to notice. They swam right into the net and suddenly it was alive, heaving violently as the salmon struggled to escape. Fingal dashed forward but was careful to keep clear of the net himself. His heart sank as he drew close to the trapped fish. He knew these salmon.

"Oh Gaffer!" he exclaimed, "Gaffer, is it you?" He was powerless to help. Gaffer was strong but the net was stronger. He heaved and fought furiously but his struggle was in vain. Bubble was there also and two other salmon from the cage, whom Fingal only knew slightly, a hen salmon called Elvira and a cock salmon called Storm. Storm was living up to his name and was fighting furiously with the strangling meshes which held him.

"It's no use," Bubble gasped at last, exhausted by the struggle. One by one, the salmon realised that the invisible thing which held them was made worse by fighting against it because the more they fought, the tighter the meshes of the net closed on them.

Fingal swam as close as he dared. It seemed desperately unfair that he should lose his friends almost as soon as he had found them again.

Bubble was first to see him. "Fingal, thank goodness, you're alive. Help us, please," she cried out, when she realised he was there.

"No, don't come near us," Gaffer warned. "We're trapped in something here. We can't get away."

"It's a net," Fingal explained dejectedly. "Men put it here to catch fish going to the river."

The old trout came up behind him. "The men will come soon and take you from the net. Fish have been known to escape when they're being removed from the net. Save your strength for that."

As usual the trout was right. A few minutes later they heard the drone of a boat engine. A fishing boat left the shore and came towards the net. At the same time the vibration of a far greater engine throbbed through the water. There was a much larger boat not very far away.

The fishermen went right to the end of the net and moved their boat along its length, lifting the meshes and removing their catch. The water stank of oil from their engine. They did not want all the fish they had caught and flung the ballan wrasse back in the water. Dead and almost dead fish floated belly up at the surface. Fingal and the trout watched. Fingal could not bear to leave till he knew the fate of his friends.

"Why do they kill fish and then throw them back in the sea?" he asked the trout. He now respected the trout's wisdom and experience. The trout had travelled this way many times before.

"They only fish for salmon and trout. They're not interested in the others but their net kills every fish that sticks in it," the trout explained.

The fishermen had just reached the section of net where Gaffer, Bubble and the other salmon were ensnared when the vibration of the large boat grew louder and the huge turbulence of its propellers made the water quiver. It was approaching at speed. Fingal and the trout withdrew to a safer distance. "The bigger boats drag nets behind them," warned the trout. "Let's keep well away from it."

This time, however, the trout was mistaken. The large boat had no net. It moved swiftly towards the fishing boat. Angry voices shouted and there was an explosive sound.

"A gun," said the trout excitedly. "The fishermen use

them sometimes to kill seals. They have rules in the world of men. The fishermen are allowed to kill trout and salmon but they may not kill seals. There are big boats, with men who enforce men's rules. I've met trout who have seen these big boats. This must be one of them."

"You think the fishermen have killed seals?" Fingal asked, puzzled at the odd rules of the world of men. How unfair that seals were allowed to live but fish could be killed.

"No, that's not the rule they have broken. I think that perhaps this invisible net may not be allowed. Look, they're dragging it out of the water." The net shuddered violently and became clearly visible as its meshes were tugged towards the surface.

There was another explosive sound of a gun and the net dropped suddenly back into place.

"The men are quarrelling," exclaimed the trout.

Overhead, the fishing boat tried to move away from the net but the big boat rammed it. It capsized, tossing its crew into the water. They moved awkwardly in the water, bobbing about clumsily at the surface. From underneath they looked ridiculous.

"What on earth are they doing now?"

The trout chuckled maliciously. "It looks as if they are fighting over the net and some of them are learning to swim."

The big boat moved forward now to rescue the fishermen from the water. Then its crew began once again to haul the monofilament net on board.

"Fight them, fight them now! Make a break for it!" Fingal and the trout urged the trapped salmon but they were lifted in the folds of the net and had no chance to escape.

Fingal waited and watched hopefully in case, by some miraculous chance, one of the captured salmon might make a break for freedom. Bit by bit the entire net was hauled from the water. There was no sign of his friends.

"We'd better go now," said the trout gently to Fingal. "This is how it is for wild fish. It's always a struggle for survival. And it's the cunning rather than the strong who survive. But at least we're free. Isn't it better to be a free fish than a pampered farm fish in a cage?"

"I suppose it is," Fingal agreed sadly.

"You must learn all you can from me before I find my river," said the trout encouragingly. "Then you'll have a better chance of survival. Remember, it's better to be cunning than to be strong . . ." He was interrupted by a flash of silver and a collision which somersaulted him through the water.

"What the . . ." Fingal began and was knocked sideways by an enthusiastic head butt.

"A little bit of luck goes a long way too," chortled the excited silver fish who was bent on tumbling Fingal and the trout upside down.

"Gaffer!" Fingal yelled in delight. "You escaped!" Then he saw the other three salmon swimming round him and he cheered again. "You all escaped?"

"You'll never believe it," said Bubble. "We were out of the sea, up in the air, and horrible it was too. We were right up in that big boat . . ."

"Gasping our last . . . " Gaffer interrupted.

"And then they put us back in the water," Bubble said excitedly, "so here we are!"

"And they were so particular about not hurting us," Gaffer said.

"They didn't want to hurt you?" The old trout was incredulous.

"One of the men kept saying, 'Gently, gently, don't hurt them,'" Bubble explained, "didn't he, Gaffer?"

"They even cut the net to make sure we wouldn't be hurt being taken out of it," added the hen salmon called Elvira.

"And then they set us free," concluded Storm, the cock salmon who had been trying to get a word in edgeways.

"Your name's Fingal, isn't it?" Elvira asked.

"Yes." Fingal was pleased that she knew his name. In the cage, among thousands of fish, it wasn't possible to know everyone's name.

"Amazing, truly amazing," said the trout, enormously impressed. "I'm an old trout and I've seen and heard many strange things in my time, but never have I heard of fish who were netted and taken into a boat and then put back in the sea. That will make a story worth telling to the other trout when I find my river."

The big boat had finished lifting the net now. With a mighty churning of water it turned and headed back in the direction from which it had come.

"Well," the trout declared with a great deal of satisfaction, "you may be sure that's one net which won't be there the next time we pass this way. Now, let's check out this river."

It was a disappointment. Once they came close enough to the full flow of river water to savour its taste the trout shook his head. "No, friends, this isn't my river. Let's go." He turned abruptly and headed south again, followed by the group of salmon.

7

The Story of the King of the Fish

For days they swam, resting only a few hours each night, sometimes on the sandy shore of a beach, sometimes in the shelter of weeds below high rocks, sometimes, as on the first night, sleeping on the coloured pebbles of a shingle shore. They no longer ate. The river was an obsession. They swam by day and by night till they were exhausted. Then they rested.

They tasted many rivers. Guided by the trout, they avoided the traps laid by men. There were many drift nets, some of them invisible, like the first one they had seen. The bag net was another insidious trap. When they came to one of these for the first time it was Fingal who spotted the net. Confident that he knew how to cope with it, he turned seaward and moved along its length. "Look out," the trout called out and Fingal turned, just in the nick of time as the fisherman above pulled rapidly on a rope and closed the bag which formed the outer end of the net.

"Whew," exclaimed Fingal, "that was a near thing. Thanks, trout."

"Never take a net for granted," warned the trout. "Men are very devious. Just when you think you've mastered their tricks, they come up with something new."

They woke next morning to the signs of an

42

approaching storm. Sea urchins which, during the calm weather, had climbed to the top of the woody stalks of laminaria sea-rods and hung like exotic blossoms among their brown fronds, were now crawling down again and finding sheltered nooks in rock crevices. The swell that precedes wind had risen with the morning tide and broke thunderously on the nearby shore. "We had better find deep water," said the trout. "There's some nasty weather on its way."

They swam west towards the approaching storm. By the time they met it they were snug and safe in deep water, under the shelter of a large shelf of rock. Fingal took the opportunity to doze. After the days of travelling he was glad of some extra rest. He was aroused by an angry voice. "Hey, you lot, what are you doing in my pad?" A large eel thrust his massive head under the rock shelf and bared his fangs ferociously.

"Get lost," the trout snarled back at him. Fingal quailed with fright. The eel looked a nasty customer. However, it must have weighed the situation and decided that a bad tempered trout and five large salmon out-matched him. He moved away, grumbling about the bad manners of certain fish who would take over another fish's pad without being invited.

"We're sheltering from the storm," Fingal explained but the eel just glared sourly at him before curling his long narrow body into a deep crevice in the rear of the rock shelf.

"Merely passing through," added the trout, "sampling the local hospitality."

"I didn't invite you," snorted the eel and he withdrew out of sight.

The storm continued throughout the day and into the night. The hours grew long and tedious. Then Gaffer had an idea. "Trout," he said, "you've lived a long life. You must have seen many things and heard many things in your time. We've never been anywhere except in our cage. We don't know the things that wild fish know. Tell us about your life so that we can learn from you."

The trout was flattered that a mighty fish like Gaffer should defer to his wisdom. "Indeed, I've lived a long life and I've seen many strange and marvellous things in my time. And I know the lore of the trout which is not so different to the lore of the salmon, for in many ways we're alike. It's told that the first trout and the first salmon created in the ocean were brothers and so it is that all salmon and trout are brothers and sisters to each other to this day."

"We're all your brothers and sisters?" exclaimed Bubble with delight. "I'm so glad we're related."

"I suppose it is rather nice," agreed the trout, flattered that Bubble wanted to claim kinship. "Would you like me to tell you the story?"

"Yes, please," the salmon said eagerly.

"Gather round me," said the trout. They gathered round and he began. "A long, long time ago, when the land and the ocean were new and the triple mother goddess, who gave birth to the earth and the sky and the sea, was still young and still beautiful . . . "

"That is the most wonderful beginning to a story that I have ever heard," murmured Elvira.

"But you've never heard a story before, have you?" Storm protested.

"No, I haven't, but it's still the most beautiful story I have ever heard," Elvira insisted.

"Please, don't interrupt," said the trout indignantly.

"Sorry."

"As I was saying," the trout resumed, "in that time long, long ago . . . " He paused and turned to Elvira. "What do you mean, you never heard a story before?"

"I never did," Elvira said.

"None of us did," said Fingal. "There was nobody to tell us stories. We all knew the same things in the cage. We were hatched together and always lived together."

"You've never heard how the salmon became the king of all the fish?"

"You mean that salmon are the king of fish?" asked Fingal, awed at the idea.

"Of course. Every fish knows that the salmon is the king of the fish. And his brother, the trout, is lord of the river."

"You mean we're royalty?" Bubble exclaimed, enormously impressed. All the salmon flexed their fins self-consciously and held themselves a little proudly as they realised their importance as monarchs among fish.

"I suppose I'd better tell you about it," said the trout. "It's part of the lore of the trout as well as the lore of the salmon. It happened in the days when the triple Goddess still ruled earth, ocean and sky, before the gods of trouble and strife had challenged her power. In that time long ago, Manannan, god of the sea, was young and giddy and much given to visiting his friends who lived on the land and in the sky, or indeed who lived anywhere other than in the sea.

"In his absence the storms came and raged furiously because there was nobody there to command them to behave themselves. The winds lashed the ocean into monstrous waves which tore the seaweeds from their rocks and drove the fish into whatever shelter they could find. So, all the year round, it was winter in the ocean. This continued till the triple goddess, who had created land and sea and sky, came to visit her creation. She saw the ocean raging. She looked for the fish and found them cowering in crevices and under rocks trying to escape the fury of the storm. Very vexed at this state of affairs, she called Manannan to her and demanded to know why he neglected his domain.

"'I've been visiting my friends on the high mountain,' he replied.

"The Goddess was angry. 'How dare you leave your kingdom without appointing somebody to take charge in your absence,' she scolded.

"Manannan was dismayed. He didn't say to the Goddess that such an idea had never occurred to him. Instead he stammered, 'Well, actually, I've been thinking about that problem . . . er . . . er . . . '

"'Yes?' said the Goddess, 'do continue.'

"'What we . . . er . . . what we need,' Manannan went on, thinking as hard and as fast as he could, 'is someone to whom I could delegate responsibility . . . you know . . . er . . . yes, I have it, we need a king of all the fish, a king who would rule the ocean in my absence.'

"'Then you had better stop thinking about it and do it,' snapped the Goddess. 'See to it at once.'

"Manannan immediately called a great meeting of all the fish and asked them to choose a king. 'I'm going away for three days to feast with my friends in the eastern valley,' he said, 'and when I return I'll ask you to choose.'

"The shark immediately announced his intention of standing for election, 'For,' he said, 'We're a large family. The tope and the dogfish and the basking shark and the grey and the white and the blue shark are all one family. We're the largest and the fiercest fish in the sea. We demand that you choose us.'

"'But I'm quite sure we outnumber the sharks,' muttered the shoals of mackerel and herring indignantly. 'All we have to do is decide which of us should lead.' They turned around to look among their number for a leader, but each time one of them turned, the entire shoal did the same thing and so they turned round and round until they were too dizzy to discuss the matter intelligently.

"'Personally,' said the crab, 'I think that I, the crab, would make an excellent king. I have a good appearance, you must admit that. And a lot of experience.'

"'Experience?' objected all the other fish, 'what experience?'

"'Well,' said the crab, 'whenever you fish make a mess I'm always the one who picks up the bits and pieces.'

"They argued all day and all night and nobody noticed that the salmon had slipped away from the meeting without saying a word. He went to the river to visit his brother, the trout. 'Manannan has told us to choose a king of all the fish, to rule when he is not around,' he told the trout.

"'Which is quite often,' said the trout, 'judging from what I've been hearing.'

"'You know how Manannan is,' sighed the salmon, 'not exactly the soul of efficiency. And his social life takes up a lot of his time. He completely forgot to invite you fish from the river to his meeting.'

"'But we're not part of his domain,' said the trout.

"'No, but the triple Goddess told him to appoint a king of the fish. Manannan will get it all wrong. You'll see a shark or a shoal of mackerel swimming up your river, claiming it as their kingdom.'

"'I see what you mean,' said the trout. 'That would be tiresome.'

"'If the river fish will vote to make me king, I promise you that I will never harm any creature in the river.'

"'How will we be certain that you will keep your promise?'

"'I will leave my children with you as hostages until they are old enough to travel to the sea. In this way you can be sure that I will never harm any of you.'

"'Very well, leave it to me,' said the trout.

"When Manannan came back at the end of his three days of feasting in the eastern valley he had to shout to make himself heard above the din of arguing fish. 'Quiet!' he yelled. 'Now, it's time to vote. Every fish must vote for the fish he chooses to be king. Who will vote first?'

"'We will,' called a voice from the edge of the crowd.

"'Who are you?' asked Manannan in astonishment for there, on the edge of the crowd were a great many fish which he had never seen before. There were trout and perch, bream and roach and many more.

"'We are the fish of the river. You can't appoint a king of the fish without consulting with us,' said the trout.

"'This is none of your business,' growled a ferocious blue shark and he bared his teeth at the river fish.

"A huge pike, almost as big as the shark, pushed his way through the crowd of smaller river fish and bared his teeth too. 'We're making it our business,' he growled back.

"'Please, please, no quarrelling,' said Manannan who wasn't quite sure if it was legal for river fish to be in his domain at all.

"Then the salmon swam forward and spoke with authority. 'I knew, Manannan, that you were in a hurry to attend to your many duties and so I took it upon myself to carry your message to the river fish, who, although they are not of your kingdom, are nevertheless fish and must have some say in the matter of who becomes king of the fish. They do have a right, don't you think? You yourself said every fish would be allowed to vote.'

"'Yes, yes . . . er . . . of course,' stuttered Manannan, not quite sure what he had said. 'Yes, of course. So I did.'

"'Let us now put the matter to a vote and choose a king,' said the trout. 'My friends and I are anxious to return to our river. Some of us are not altogether comfortable in your salty water.'

"'Yes, let's do that,' agreed Manannan. 'Please, carry on.'

"The squid, who were best at counting because of their many tentacles, were appointed to tally the vote. The sharks, naturally, voted for the sharks. The mackerel and the herring made a great deal of noise and dashed to and fro throughout the meeting but when their votes were counted it was discovered that every fish had voted for itself. When the salmon's votes were toted up, all the river fish gave him their support and so the salmon became the king of the fish and his brother, the trout, lord of the river.

"That is why, to this day, the salmon visits the river every year and leaves his children there to grow up. And because the trout is his brother, the trout is free to leave his river, live in the sea and become a sea trout.

"So you see," concluded the old sea trout, "you are the kings of the fish and we are the lords of the river. We are the aristocracy among fish."

"You have come a long way from your river domain," said Gaffer curiously. "Do many trout travel as you do or only some?"

"I'm a sea trout," replied the old trout. "For us trout it's a matter of choice. We can go upstream and live in the rivers, lakes and streams all our lives or we can stay in the river estuary where the water is both fresh and salt or we can go to the sea. I'm a sea trout because I was brought up a sea trout and I know of no better way of living than the life of a sea trout. I lead an adventurous, dangerous life but I also see a great deal of the world and meet many strange and remarkable creatures. I think I would find the life of a river or lake trout dreadfully tedious. I like variety."

"That was a really interesting story," said Elvira. "Do you know any more like that?"

"Oh lots and lots," said the trout complacently. "Sea trout are great travellers. We can tell many fine tales."

"Travellers!" interrupted a scornful voice. "You trout think you are travellers! You travel a few miles up the coastline and then a few miles back down again and you call yourselves travellers. You trout are only trippers. Tourists!" An eel uncurled himself from the niche in the rock where he had hidden and emerged, stretching sinuously almost the full length of the rock shelf.

"We are great travellers," said the trout, not at all dismayed by the rudeness of the eel's interruption, "within our range, that is. But I've heard that you eels are truly the greatest voyagers of all."

"Yes," said the eel, pleased that trout had not contradicted him, "we are the children of the great serpent mother goddess who once ruled the earth and made it fruitful but was driven into the sea by the war gods who seized the earth from her and plundered its fruits."

"Tell us about your travels, great eel," asked the trout

in a very respectful tone. He deliberately flattered the
eel for it was not often that an eel would speak to any
but his own kind. In the river estuary they were
regarded as mysterious creatures, endowed with the
magical powers of their serpent goddess mother. What
a tale he would have to tell to the dull little stay-at-
home river trout if the eel would tell him about his
travels.

The eel, perhaps because he was bored with the
endless hours of sheltering from the storm, proved
quite talkative. "We eels," he began, "as you can see,
are quite unlike other fish. We have the serpent shape
of our great mother goddess and when we choose, we
can leave the water and cross land. Like you trout and
salmon, we live in both fresh and salt water. We have
the knowledge and powers bestowed on us by our
serpent mother and her wisdom and cunning."

"Where were you born?" asked the trout. This was
the greatest mystery of all. Some fish said that eels were
created from the sun's heat when it shone upon the
flooding of the sacred river Nilus and others maintained
that eels bred of mud. Then there were those who
insisted that they bred from a magical dew which fell
upon certain rivers and lakes in the month of May.

Certainly the trout had never seen an eel spawn.
Everyone knew that eels left their river to live in the sea
and never returned. Yet their young appeared in the
rivers in springtime although the adult eels never
returned to spawn like the trout and the salmon. It was
very peculiar.

"You have seen where the sun sets in the west?" the
eel began.

"You mean that great pool of red and gold where the
ocean meets the sky?" said Elvira.

"Beyond that pool of red and gold is more ocean and beyond that more ocean again and beyond that is a sea where the burning sun sleeps all night. Sargasso weed lies thickly on the surface and underneath, the water is warm and full of burning light. That is the spawning ground of the eels. It is there that we are born, in the realm of the sunset. It is from there that we must make our way to the rivers of our parents, guided only by the wisdom with which the serpent goddess has endowed us."

"But how do you find your way when you have never seen your river?" Fingal asked. He felt that the eel's wisdom would help him recognise his own river when he came to it. If what the eel told them was true, then the eel could find his river without ever having been there before.

"Every fish knows his river when he comes to it. He will taste its waters and know that this is home."

"Home," Fingal echoed. Of course, his own river would be home and he would know it.

The eel continued his story. "The Sargasso sea is the source of the warm current that drifts eastwards from the Gulf to meet the sunrise. The young eels are carried by this current across the vastness of the ocean till it drifts northward to these waters. Then we enter our rivers as elvers, only three inches long, an inch for each year of our voyage."

"That is amazing, truly amazing," exclaimed the trout. He made a mental note of the name of the Sargasso sea, where the sun sleeps all night. What a story!

"The rest you know," said the eel. "We grow to adulthood in the river and then, during the first moon of autumn, the serpent goddess calls us back to the sea, not all of us, only those whom she has marked with the silver of the ocean, for you must have seen how the eels who go to sea turn silver while those who stay in the river keep the colour of the river mud."

"Yes, I've seen that," the trout agreed.

"When the moon is full we gather together, in our thousands, and bid farewell forever to the river, for we never return there."

"And have you been back yet to the Sargasso sea?" asked the trout.

"Not yet," said the eel, "I must live here in this cold green sea until it is my turn to follow the burning light of the sunset."

"How will you know when it is your turn?"

"My turn will come when the goddess calls me."

"That will indeed be a greater journey than any journey a trout will make," said the trout, enormously impressed and delighted to have discovered the mystery of the eel's spawning place.

"That was almost as good a story as the story the trout told," Elvira added enthusiastically.

"Almost! You don't know much about stories, do you?" said the eel, glaring balefully at her. With as much dignity as he could muster he curled himself back into the crevice in the rock and disappeared from view.

"Shush, Elvira," whispered the other salmon. She always managed to say the wrong thing.

8

Attacked by Seals

When they awoke next morning, the storm had passed. The sea was misty, clouded with the debris which the waves had torn from the seabed and fragments of many coloured seaweed were suspended in the water.

"Time to go," said the trout, turning south and swimming off once more. The salmon followed. They were still far out at sea when they tasted a current of fresh water flowing in its own channel on the salt sea. "It's a river," cheered the salmon delightedly.

"It's a very great river," said the trout and he leapt high out of the water in his excitement, then followed the channel in the direction of its source.

"Careful, trout, be careful," shouted Gaffer when the trout seemed bent on swimming headlong into a driftnet which was anchored across the flood of fresh water.

"What's wrong with him?" worried Fingal. The trout was usually the canniest and most cautious of them all. This morning he was positively careless. Fingal did not have long to wait to find out what was the matter.

They approached a sandbar where the remaining surge of the previous day's storm turned to rolling surf. Its thunder could be heard a long way out to sea. North of the sandbar was the river channel and beyond that, a wide expanse of muddy estuary. The trout leaped again.

He flung himself into the air and thrashed the surface of the water with his tail, spinning himself forward in a crazy dance.

"Trout, what are you doing?" Fingal shouted, "come back here!"

"It's my river, this is my river," the trout called back to him and continued to leap and dance. Then he dived back down to Fingal. "Taste it. It's my home river. Don't you recognise it?"

"No, I don't," Fingal answered. He turned to the other salmon. "Do any of you taste . . . home?" They shook their heads. Fingal turned back to the trout. "I don't think this is our river."

"Do you suppose we could stay anyway?" Elvira suggested.

"Could we?" Fingal asked the trout, "I don't want to leave you."

"That would never do," said the trout, too filled with the joy of finding his river to express much regret. "You would still long for your own river. You must go on and find it. I have to leave you now. This is my home."

"But we are your friends now. Have you any friends here?" Fingal asked with concern. He was afraid the old trout would be lonely when they left him. He remembered how lonely he had been when he first escaped from the fish farm cage.

The trout understood his concern. "Don't worry about me," he said. "First I'll spend a few days looking up old friends in the estuary and then I'll find the tributary stream where I was spawned myself. I always go back there, for old time's sake. I'll meet a great many of my own relations in that stream and then," he reddened a little around the gills, "I may have a little romantic interlude with an old sweetheart of mine . . . "

"You're blushing, Trout," exclaimed Elvira.

"Well, why shouldn't I blush?" retorted the trout. "You'll be a little red around the gills yourself when you've been up your river for a while. Just you wait and see."

He said goodbye and dashed away, skirting the pounding surf on the sandbar and following the deep channel into the river.

"What now?" wondered Bubble. The salmon looked at each other, at a loss to know who would lead, now that the trout was gone.

Gaffer turned south. "Let's go," he called to them and swam quickly away. They all hurried to catch up with him.

The previous day's storm had passed but there was still enough wind to whip the surface water into white crests. Below the surface, the water was agitated by the last of the storm's swell and visibility was reduced to a few feet. For the salmon, these were ideal conditions for travelling. They swam quickly all day and journeyed on after the last light of day turned the grey sea to gold before black night descended. Through the night they continued their journey and paused to rest for a while just before dawn.

At daybreak Gaffer nudged them awake. "Let's go," he cried out and turned towards the south. They followed eagerly. Fingal followed too, but with a vague feeling of uneasiness. They swam quickly forward but again and again he felt impelled to stop and look back in the direction from which they had come. Then, satisfied that there was nothing there, he hurried onwards to catch up with the others.

"Come on Fingal," Bubble called to him impatiently. "Don't dawdle."

Gaffer stopped and waited for him. "Are you tired, Fingal?" he asked, "we can stop for a rest if you want."

"No, I'm not tired," he said, "it's just . . . " He peered into the misty green ocean behind.

Then Gaffer too, stiffened all over and held himself poised for flight. "I feel it now . . . I know what you mean, there's something there. Let's take cover." They swam down deep into the steep banks of weed at the sea bed and waited. A moment later four fish flashed by, slender and green against the surface light.

"Salmon?" exclaimed Fingal.

"It looks like that," Gaffer agreed and darted forward to intercept them. Fingal followed.

"Hey, you lot," Gaffer challenged, swimming across their path, "what do you mean by following us?"

The four fish stopped to stare curiously at him. "Hello," said the biggest of the group, a large, full-grown hen salmon.

Fingal swam up to them. "What's the big idea? Why are you following us?" he demanded.

"We're not following you," replied the smallest of the four fish. She was a dainty little salmon grilse, with silver tips on her fins. Just like Silverfin, Fingal remembered with a pang of regret and was sorry he had spoken so aggressively.

"We're on our way to our river. Where are you lot headed?" said the largest of the four.

"Sorry," Gaffer apologised, feeling a bit foolish. "We thought you were something sneaking up on us. We could sense that something was following close behind us."

"Well, that's not unusual," said the large salmon.

"There are a lot of salmon travelling to their rivers at this time of year. Haven't you ever travelled to your river before?"

"No, never," said Bubble. She had gathered courage and followed Fingal and Gaffer to inspect the newcomers. "This is our first time. We escaped from a fish farm."

"Oh, you're farm fish," said the big salmon. "Ah yes, that explains a great deal. I wondered how so many very big fish came to be travelling together."

"Don't wild fish grow big?" asked Elvira. She had joined them and was circling round the wild fish, observing them with interest.

"We do if we get the chance," said the third wild fish who had not spoken till now. He was a medium sized cock salmon with a jagged scar at the corner of his mouth. "Our life is full of hazards. We meet with danger every day, especially when we travel to our river. And even when we reach our river there are traps and lures to decoy us to our deaths. Not many of us survive."

"What happened to your mouth?" Elvira asked.

The scarred fish turned his head sharply away.

"Elvira, must you always say the wrong thing," Fingal muttered to her.

"Sorry." Elvira swam round the offended fish and butted him gently. "I'm not very discreet. I'm Elvira, sometimes called motormouth. What's your name?"

"Motormouth!" chuckled the scarred fish. He didn't seem offended any more. "That name suits you all right. I'm Duff."

"What did happen?" Elvira asked. "I'm not just being a motormouth. I really do want to know. We don't know much about things out here in the wild ocean.

We didn't learn much in our cage."

"I was hooked by a man, a river angler. He had a lure dancing on the water's surface. It was so pretty, I wanted to play with it and then, suddenly, I was caught on a hook. Its barbed point bedded itself into my mouth . . . "

"Ouch," said Elvira sympathetically.

"Luckily for me he was not a very skilful angler. When he pulled too eagerly on his line he held it nicely taut so that I could strike it with my tail and break it. An angler must play a salmon and let us swim away with his line if he hopes to catch us. So I escaped. A little wiser for the experience. It took me most of the season to rub that hook out of my lip. I saw many of my companions hooked and caught on that same river journey. I keep well away from those pretty lures now."

The salmon introduced themselves. The newcomers were the large hen salmon whose name was Rocky, the little grilse called Coral Bud, a sickly, underweight fish with a whitish growth near one of his gills whose name was Engus and Duff, the medium sized cock salmon who had already made friends with Elvira.

Elvira was full of questions. "Where have you travelled from? Which is your river? Is it far?"

Gaffer circled uneasily, anxious to be on his way again. "Let's go," he said, turning south and speeding away. The wild fish followed without question. "Are you coming with us?" Fingal asked but the wild salmon were already swimming alongside them.

Elvira swam beside Duff, still eagerly questioning him. The little grilse swam alongside Fingal. "You're such a great big salmon," she said admiringly, "do you mind if I swim with you? This my first time too, to go to the river." Fingal was flattered. She seemed a sweet little fish and her silver-tipped fins reminded him of Silverfin.

It was pleasant to travel with the wild fish. Duff and Rocky had been this way before in previous migrations and knew the shoreline. Towards nightfall they led the others to a sheltered bay near a freshwater stream where they rested for a while and tasted the fresh water. They knew it was not their river when they had first tasted it a long way off shore but came inshore to splash and frolic in it anyway. A fisherman had stretched a bag net near the mouth of the stream but the tide was full and the net unattended. "Can you do this," challenged Rocky, flinging herself over the back rope of the net. The corks on the rope bobbed in a row along its length.

"Of course I can," shouted Storm, flinging himself over it too.

"Don't be stupid," Gaffer said angrily. "Nets are dangerous. Keep away from them. Don't take unnecessary risks."

"Are you afraid?" Rocky jeered.

"Yes, I'm afraid you'll make a mistake and get caught in it. Now, stop fooling about. It's time for us to move on. Let's go." He led the way along the length of the net and once clear of it, turned south as usual.

"Spoil sport," Rocky grumbled but followed nevertheless.

They travelled through the night. Gaffer kept a careful watch ahead for nets and led the group of salmon cautiously round them. He occasionally stopped to allow Engus, the thin wild salmon, to rest because he seemed to have trouble keeping up. "I want to see my river just once," Engus said, "just once more."

"What's wrong with him?" Fingal asked Coral Bud.

"He's sick," Coral Bud whispered. "Don't let him hear you. He doesn't like us to speak of his disease. Many salmon died of it last season. He wants to see his river just one more time."

Fingal felt sorry for him. He hoped he would be able to complete the journey to his river. However, Engus never did see his river again.

It was just before dawn that a new enemy struck. Several sleek shining black seals shot through the water. The wild salmon were quicker to react to the danger than the farm fish. Fingal had often seen seals through the meshes of the cage. It seemed so long ago now. But he had not realised that seals posed any danger to salmon because the meshes had always protected them from attack. Now, however, they were exposed to their onslaught.

"Seals!" screamed little Coral Bud at his side and she swam as fast as she could, with Fingal hurrying alongside. They passed Engus.

"Wait for me," he cried, making a desperate attempt to swim faster but falling rapidly behind.

The group of salmon swam furiously onward. Fingal sensed the kill when one of the seals struck Engus and dropped back out of the chase. The other seals continued their pursuit of the salmon. Suddenly, directly ahead of them, a net loomed, cutting off their escape. Gaffer looked back at the approaching seals. There would not be time to travel round the net. They were trapped, an easy prey.

"Don't leave me," whimpered Coral Bud.

Fingal remembered how helpless he had been when Silverfin was killed. He braced himself to meet the seals. He would not give up without a fight. The seals rushed towards them. Then an idea struck him. There was an escape, if only they acted quickly enough.

"Follow me," he said to Coral Bud and rushed towards the surface. He saw the line of corks which marked the back rope. "Jump, quickly, jump now," he shouted and flung himself across the rope. He landed safely just beyond the net and Coral Bud splashed down into the water beside him. The other fish followed. The seals, blinded by the eagerness of their pursuit, did not see the net. They rushed headlong into it and were quickly entangled in its meshes.

"Fingal, you are a genius," said Coral Bud, looking gleefully at the trapped seals.

"Idiots," Storm jeered in delight.

"Where's Engus?" Elvira asked. They fell silent as they realised that Engus was missing.

"He was behind us," said Fingal, "but I think he was caught."

Duff looked sad. "I'll miss him. We hatched in the same stream and we always travelled together. I wish he could have seen his river just once more."

"It had to happen sometime," Coral Bud tried to comfort him. "He was growing weaker every day."

"Come on," Rocky urged. "Keep swimming. Those seals will not be trapped for very long. They have sharp teeth and will cut their way out of the net."

The salmon regrouped and swam quickly away, still bearing south. On their landward side the sea turned gold and then blue-green as the sunrise proclaimed a new day.

9

The Story of the Tinker

They continued their journey, the low shoreline to the east giving way to steep cliffs which rose high above the ocean surface and shelved deeply below it. The water there, in the shadow of the sheer mountain cliff face above, was icy cold and dark. The salmon were exhilarated by the cold and dived deep into the murky depths, all the way down to where large sour-faced turbot skulked on the sea-bottom.

South of the cliffs they came to another river. Its estuary was long and narrow, with a rocky shore on its north side. A stone pier extended halfway across the entrance to the estuary, forming a sheltered harbour where many boats lay moored. The water reeked of oil and the sandy bottom was littered with rubbish.

"Man," said Duff critically, "he fouls every place he goes. Just look at this mess. Even the tide can't shift this lot."

It was not their river but the wild salmon wanted to pay a courtesy visit. There were several groups of salmon in the estuary and Duff and Rocky seemed either to have met them previously or to have met some acquaintance of theirs. It was evident that wild salmon made a wide circle of acquaintance on their winter migrations. The farm fish listened intently as Duff and Rocky chatted with a group of salmon whom they had met while wintering off the Greenland coast.

"Were you bothered much by nets?" asked one aged cock salmon with a hooked lower jaw.

"Oh yes, there were a lot of them. We had to be very careful," said Duff.

"When I was young," the old salmon reminisced, "I knew lots of old fish who had known fish when they were young, who remembered a time when there were no nets in the winter feeding grounds. Men had not found out where we spent the winter. Aye, those were the days. Now, the men are everywhere. Here's our river, we have to go up it, but if we go on the morning tide the anglers will be there to take us out of it and if we go on the night tide there will be poachers with their nets. It's only a little river. It's no easy matter getting to our spawning beds. But there it is. That's the struggle of life. And what is life without a struggle, as the tinker would say."

The old salmon chatted away to himself, not really interested in whether or not anybody was listening. Fingal, however, listened attentively. He knew from what he had learned of the wisdom of the trout that there was much to be learned from an old fish. "The tinker?" he echoed. "What is a tinker?"

"You mean, who is the tinker," the old fish corrected him. "The tinker is the trickiest, most cunning salmon in sea or river. No fisherman can catch him for," the salmon dropped his voice to a confidential whisper, "he is cleverer than the devil himself."

"The devil? What is that? Or should I ask who?"

"You may well ask." said the old fish earnestly. "The devil is the spirit of wickedness in man."

"And you say there is a salmon cleverer than the devil?" asked Fingal in awe.

"For goodness sake, Fingal," said Coral Bud

impatiently, "don't listen to such nonsense. Old fish are always full of tall stories."

"This is a true story," said the old salmon sternly. "I know it's true for I heard it from an old fish when I was young and he heard it from an old fish when he was young."

"And where did he hear it?" Coral Bud demanded, still incredulous.

"Ha! I thought you'd ask that. He heard it told by a man to his child. He listened as he lay in a pool near the river bank where they were sitting."

"What is a child?" asked Coral Bud, more impressed now.

"A child is a man-smolt," said the old fish, "and this is the story as I heard it when I was young, from a very old salmon who heard it when he was young from . . . "

"That's all right, we know that bit," said Coral Bud, "tell us the story."

"Hasn't anyone ever told you that it's rude to interrupt your elders?" said the old fish. "If you're not interested . . . "

"Shush," Fingal said to Coral Bud. "Please continue," he said to the old fish. "This is all very interesting to me. I'm a farm salmon and I know hardly any salmon stories. Please do continue."

The old fish continued, gratified to find a listener who really wanted to listen. "Well, there was once a man who was a tinker, that is, he made tin cans like those tin cans which you see lying there on the sea bottom at the harbour. He worked with his hands and his bag of tools to make these cans, though why men make cans in order to throw them into the sea, I don't understand. The old fish who told me the story knew nothing of that.

"Now, this tinker had great trouble with his bag of tools because whenever any other man wanted to use a hammer or a saw or a piece of wire he borrowed it from the tinker's tool bag. The tinker was a poor man and did not have the money to replace what was taken from his bag so he made a poor enough living at his trade. 'But,' he always said when times were hard, 'what is life without a struggle?'

"All the same, it was hard for the tinker to be patient when people borrowed his few tools from his tool bag and neglected to return them. 'The devil take my soul,' he swore one day when he found his iron anvil was gone missing from the tool bag, for he could not work at all without his anvil. With that there was a flash and a terrible crash and there was the devil himself standing before him.

"'How much?' asked the devil, eager to strike a bargain at once.

"'Who are you?' asked the tinker, greatly dismayed at the company he found himself in and knowing well enough what the answer would be.

"'I am the devil, and if I am not mistaken you have just offered to give me your soul,' said the wicked fellow eagerly.

"'You don't think you can have it for nothing,' said the tinker, for being a tinker he knew how to drive a good bargain.

"'I'll give you three wishes in exchange for your soul,' said the devil, 'and I'll be in no hurry to collect. You may keep your soul for as long as you wish. Not until you ask me to, will I come to fetch what is mine.'

"The tinker pondered the matter. He was a poor man and had worked hard all his life. Now he could be rich beyond his wildest dreams. The devil's offer seemed ridiculously generous. He would not have to give up his soul to him till it suited himself. 'Will you give me a purse full of money which will always be full no matter how much money I take out of it?' he asked.

"'Done,' said the devil and a great purse of money weighed heavily in the tinker's pocket.

"'Will you return to my tool bag all the tools that have ever been borrowed from it?' said the tinker.

"'Done,' said the Devil and immediately the tool bag bulged and overflowed with all the tools the tinker had ever owned.

"'Will you put a charm on the bag now, so that nothing that is in it can be taken out of it except by myself?'

"'Done,' said the devil, 'no one but yourself can take anything out of it now. Do we have a bargain?'

"'Done,' said the tinker and he was well pleased that he had the best of the bargain.

"He went at once and bought himself fine clothes. He built a house with a window for every day in the year. He married a beautiful young wife and thought he was the happiest man in the land. They feasted day and night and the tinker did not work any more for he had all the money he could possibly need.

Yet, as time went by, he grew discontented. He longed for the wandering life on the open road and one day, when the longing grew too much for him, he took his tool bag from the corner where it had lain gathering dust all this time. Then he kissed his wife goodbye, gave her his magic purse full of money for the housekeeping and set off journeying.

"'Any old pots or pans for mending, any knives for sharpening, ma'am?' he asked at the first house on the road.

"The woman of the house looked at him in

astonishment. 'Old pots and pans? Oh sir, what do you mean?'

"'I'm a tinker, ma'am,' said the tinker, 'and I've come to mend your pots and pans.'

"The woman began to laugh to think that this fine gentleman wanted to mend her pots and pans. She called her husband to share in the joke.

"'The devil take my soul,' swore the tinker, indignantly, 'but I'm a tinker by trade, no matter about my fine clothes . . . ' He did not finish what he meant to say for there was a flash of lightning and a crash and the devil stood before him.

"'Well,' said the devil, 'aren't you in a great hurry to go down below. I thought you would take a year or two at least before availing of our hospitality. But now you've called on me to take your soul, I'll be glad to oblige.'

"The tinker realised he had made a terrible blunder. However, he didn't let the devil see his dismay. 'My soul is yours,' he said, handing it over, 'but before I go with you, I must mend this woman's pots and pans. I am not a man to break a promise.'

"'Very well,' said the devil, putting the tinker's soul into his pocket, having first checked that there was no hole in his pocket where it might slip out. 'I'll let you mend her pots and then you must come with me.'

"The tinker took his anvil from the bag and his heavy mallet. The woman of the house, a little bit shaken to find the devil as well as a finely dressed tinker at her door, went without argument to her kitchen and brought back a couple of battered saucepans.

"The tinker took one of the saucepans and examined it carefully. 'Hand me that hammer out of my toolbag,' he said to the devil, 'the one with a corkscrew handle on it.'

"The devil looked in the toolbag. 'I don't see any hammer with a corkscrew handle,' he said.

"'It must be down in the bottom of the bag. Take a look and see,' the tinker insisted.

"The devil put his head into the bag to look. As he did so the tinker leapt forward, pushed the devil into the bag and closed the neck of it. 'Let me out,' shouted the devil but he was trapped in the toolbag. He himself had enchanted it so that only the tinker would have the power to take anything out of it. 'Let me out and I will give you anything that you ask for,' he cried.

"'Will you give me back my soul?' asked the tinker.

"'No.'

"'Then stay where you are.' The tinker set about tying the neck of the bag with a piece of twine.

"'All right, all right, I'll give you back your soul," howled the devil, knowing that he had been outwitted.

"The tinker opened the bag and lifted the devil out by the scruff of his neck. 'I'll have my soul back now, if you don't mind,' he said and held out his hand.

"Reluctantly, the devil gave it back to him. 'Much good it may do you,' he grumbled.

"'How's that?" asked the tinker.

"'A man's soul cannot go back into his body once it has come out of it,' said the devil. You will have to choose a new shape.'

"The tinker considered the problem. 'I will be a salmon,' he decided, 'because a salmon leads a fine wandering life.'

"There was a river close by, a clear, fast-running salmon stream. The tinker plunged into it and immediately became a silver salmon with a broad black back. And because a man's soul is immortal, the tinker lives to this day, roaming between the river and the

sea, wandering the ocean in winter and returning to
the river, sometimes in springtime, sometimes in
summer, sometimes in autumn, for he is to be found
in any of the great or little salmon rivers. There is no
salmon in river or sea more cunning or clever than the
tinker for he is the only creature who ever outwitted
the devil himself."

The old salmon nodded sagely as he ended his story.
"And that's the truth," he said, "For I heard that story from
a very old salmon when I was young who heard it from
an old salmon when he was young who heard it . . . "

"I know," said Coral Bud, "you told us that bit
already."

"Did I?" The old fish pondered a moment. "Yes, so I
did. So I did."

"That's a very fine story," said Fingal. "Does it have a
moral?"

"A moral? I couldn't say. The fish who told it to me
said nothing about any moral." He thought for a
moment. "Still, I'm an old fish and I've seen the ways
of the world. If there's a lesson to be learned from that
story, I suppose I am old enough and wise enough to
figure it out. Yes, I suppose the moral might be that
you shouldn't let your tongue run away with you. You
young fish have far too much to say, you know. Hardly
let an old fish get a word in edgeways. Or maybe the
lesson is, that you shouldn't put your head into a place
unless you're sure you'll get it out of it again, or
maybe . . . " He rambled on, quite forgetting that he
had an audience. Coral Bud nudged Fingal and they
slipped away, leaving the old fish solemnly moralising
to himself while the tide flooded gently around him
and bore him forward towards his native stream.

10

A Baby Seal and An Otter

The tide was full and lapping against the sandbanks where the river channel bent to the south shore when Fingal and his friends left the estuary. Outside, the sea was calm. Splintered sunlight pierced the surface and made every living thing below languid and weary. The salmon swam onwards, slowly now, with Gaffer still leading. At last night fell. The sea felt cool again and they were no longer dazzled by the brightness of the sun. Now they could travel quickly, always in search of their river. Towards morning land loomed ahead of them.

"Go carefully now," warned Rocky, swimming forward to accompany Gaffer. "That is seal island ahead of us, the breeding ground of the seals. We must bear well to the west if we are to pass safely. I remember this place from last year. We lost several of our group here."

Gaffer turned west and headed for the open sea. It was not yet light but in the distance they heard the sound of boat engines. There were men not very far away. Gaffer led more slowly, watching carefully for nets. Since becoming a wild fish he had learned that where there were men there was always danger. They swam cautiously, circling wide around the island.

Fingal was the first of the salmon to sense death

nearby, sending its impact almost imperceptibly through the ocean. Somewhere, not far away, there was blood and through the water passed the shock-waves of creatures struggling, distressed and in pain. The fish paused, bewildered. They had experienced killing at the salmon farm and they had seen killing by men and by seals since then, but this was different. While they hesitated, wondering which direction to take, three black shapes shot towards them in the water.

"Seals!" Coral Bud screamed. The salmon turned and sped back the way they had come but after a minute they stopped, bewildered once more.

"Where did they go?" Gaffer puzzled. The seals had not pursued them. And yet they had passed so close to them that they must have seen them.

"Perhaps they weren't hungry," Fingal suggested.

"Seals are always hungry," said Rocky, peering suspiciously into the water around her as if she expected a seal suddenly to appear.

"Maybe something is chasing them," said Duff. "Seals must have enemies too."

Fingal remembered something the trout had told him. "Sometimes men kill seals. It's not allowed by their own rules but sometimes they do it anyway."

"Let's get out of here," said Gaffer. The smell of death was intensifying all around them. They swam hurriedly towards the south again. As they passed close to the southerly tip of the island Fingal heard explosive sounds. He had heard that sound before, on the day that Gaffer and the other farm fish had been rescued by the big ship from the net where they were caught.

"Guns," he said excitedly, "the men have guns. I can hear them."

A disturbance in the water nearby caught his attention.

A very small silver-grey seal came into view, swimming furiously and occasionally rushing to the surface for air. He saw the salmon and made for them. The salmon backed away. "Help," cried the small seal. "Help — they're killing us!"

"Let's go," said Gaffer and they all turned quickly and swam away.

The small seal followed, paddling furiously with his ridiculously clumsy flippers and his heavy tail. "Wait for me," he called after them.

"Go back," Fingal said to him as kindly as he could. He could see that this seal was only a baby. "You can't come with us. We're salmon, you're a seal. We're enemies."

"I can't go back," the little seal whimpered, "they'll kill me."

"What's happening back there?" Coral Bud asked.

Gaffer turned back to urge Fingal and Coral Bud onwards. "Come on you two. We can't hang about here. It isn't safe."

"Just one minute," said Coral Bud.

The seal surfaced for air, then dived back down to them again. Fingal had never seen a seal up close before. Its funny little whiskered face and its big protruding eyes made it look inoffensive, but his recollection of the seal attack in which Engus was killed was too fresh in his memory for him to feel very kindly towards any seal, even a baby one.

"Sorry, we have to go. Come on you two," Gaffer said and swam away. Fingal and Coral Bud followed.

"Wait. Come back!" the seal called and swam furiously after them.

Fingal and the other salmon swam on but it was difficult to ignore the seal who kept following them and pleading for them to wait. Finally Coral Bud stopped and waited. Fingal dropped back too. Gaffer circled, thrashing his tail in irritation.

"We can't leave him," Coral Bud said, "he's only a baby. Please, Gaffer, wait for him."

Gaffer grudgingly paused and let the seal catch up with them. "You can come with us a little way but then you will have to go and find your own kind. We don't want you."

"But I have nobody else," the seal said and broke into a hoarse wailing which startled a passing pollack so that he darted for cover into a clump of laminaria weed. The pollack's flight frightened several mottled pink and purple sea anemones. They withdrew their tentacles and curled themselves into jelly blobs.

"Be quiet," Gaffer said. "If you don't stop making that noise we'll go away and leave you here."

The baby seal stifled his sobs and surfaced once more for air.

"What on earth will we do with him?" asked Duff. "It's the most ridiculous thing I've ever heard of, a baby seal travelling with salmon."

"But he's asked us for help," Rocky said solicitously. "He's probably lost his mother."

The seal dived back to them again. He floated glumly, looking from one salmon to the other waiting to see what they would decide to do with him.

"What happened on the island?" Coral Bud asked him.

The seal's mouth quivered and he seemed about to convulse with sobs again. "The men came," he said.

"Yes, we saw them," Coral Bud said gently. "And then what happened?"

"They came down to the nursery rocks where the

mothers and the babies were and started killing."

"With guns?" Fingal asked.

"Yes, with guns. We dashed for the sea. There was blood everywhere, on the rocks and in the water. They killed my mother." The small seal looked helpless and forlorn.

The salmon looked at each other. Gaffer spoke. "I suppose you could travel with us till we come to another seal colony." It was ludicrous but now that they had let the baby seal tell his story it would be difficult to abandon him. "You will have to keep up with us, no dilly dallying."

The seal found it difficult to keep up. He needed to surface for air at shorter and shorter intervals. Fingal and Coral Bud swam with him and urged him along but it soon became obvious that he would have to rest. They led him towards the shore and directed him to a patch of shingle just beyond the shoreline where he could sleep.

The salmon dozed fitfully during the night. They felt restless. They were too close to their river now to be able to take time to rest. It was a relief when day broke and the baby seal splashed and tumbled at the surface to let them know he was awake again. However he was still not ready to go. "I'm hungry," he announced.

"What do you usually feed on?" Rocky asked him.

"My mother nursed me on milk. And sometimes she brought me fish."

"Yes, well you hardly expect us to feed you fish, do you?" snapped Gaffer. He was vexed at every new delay.

The small seal nuzzled him. "Actually, you smell really delicious," he said wistfully.

"Here, mind what you're doing," Gaffer said indignantly, shrugging him off. "I'm not your breakfast."

"Have you ever had mussels?" Fingal offered hopefully, remembering how the ballan wrasse ate mussels from the rocks. The seal had teeth too, like the wrasse. He might be able to eat them.

The seal was willing to try. They found a rock covered with small mussels but the seal was unable to extract anything edible from them. "That's not food," he said, finally giving up and surfacing for air.

Rocky suggested worms. "Lots of fish eat worms. I've seen them nosing on sandy shores for them. Personally, I've never had a taste for them but I understand that trout find them quite delicious."

After a brief search of a patch of sand an unfortunate worm showed its head and Rocky tugged it out of his hole. "Well, baby seal," she asked when the seal had nibbled it tentatively.

"Disgusting," he said. "Gross. I'm glad I'm not a trout. But I do like eating trout."

Gaffer pretended not to hear. Then Fingal had an idea. "I know where we'll find breakfast for you. Follow me." He turned and swam south. There was fresh water nearby, not a lot, just enough to tell a passing salmon that there was a stream somewhere not far ahead. And where there was a fresh water stream there would be a net, probably unattended at this early hour. Fingal was right. In a short while they saw a wall of net stretched ahead. It had obviously been unattended all night. A shoal of mackerel had passed that way and left some of its number in the meshes. They were caught by the gills and stuck out rigidly. Scavenging crabs had already climbed the net and were feasting on the dead mackerel. The seal needed no invitation. He rushed at the net and gobbled several mackerel, leaving their heads still in the meshes.

"What if he gets stuck?" Coral Bud worried. "I'd hate to see the fishermen catch him."

However that was no danger to the seal. He jammed a flipper briefly in a mesh and tore the net savagely, leaving an enormous hole. Then he surfaced for air and hurried back down to make up for not having eaten the day before. In the process he tore several more holes in the net. The salmon were gleeful. They swam through the holes instead of going round the net. "I suppose seals can sometimes be good for something," said Gaffer grudgingly.

They continued to swim south but the seal slowed them down again. He had eaten so much that he could not swim quickly and had to surface again and again for air. By evening they had covered considerably less than their usual distance and Gaffer was growing increasingly impatient. Night would fall soon and the baby seal would have to sleep again. They found a grey, boulder-strewn shore in an inlet, closed on all sides by high cliffs, where he could sleep undisturbed.

The seal had just gone ashore when he leaped back into the water, pursued by an indignant, sharp nosed, whiskered animal. "How dare you come on to my shore. Off with you. Scram!" He was a long, slender creature, four legged, with reddish brown fur and a grey underbelly. He propelled himself angrily in the water with his large broad tail. "Scat", he said to the seal and quivered all over with indignation.

"What's that?" asked Fingal, startled by the apparition.

"An otter," exclaimed Duff. "I've often seen them in the river but never in the sea."

"Ah, the river, you know the river?" said the otter, turning to see who had spoken.

"Yes, we know the river," said Duff. "Have we met there?" He couldn't be sure. One otter looked much like another.

"Well, I've met salmon there," said the otter. "I've personally been acquainted with many salmon. But you know how it is, I can't remember any salmon in particular, one salmon looks much like another, you know."

"I suppose it must seem that way to you," murmured Duff. "I had no idea that otters migrated to the sea."

"Migrate? Did you say migrate?" The otter bristled, outraged at the idea.

"Didn't you migrate?"

"Certainly not. I was perfectly happy on my riverbank. What a sweet, lovely riverbank it was," he said mournfully. "My holt was there, such a fine holt."

"Holt?" asked Elvira.

"A holt is an otter's residence," said the otter. "Don't you know anything, young salmon?"

"This is her first time to go back to the river," Rocky placated him. "You're the first otter she's ever seen."

"Well, I suppose, youth is the only excuse for ignorance," said the otter philosophically. "I miss the river. I miss it so much."

"Why don't you go back?" asked Duff.

"Impossible. There are interlopers. Low, cunning fellows. Nasty, brutish, vicious fellows. They took my fishing grounds, overran my riverbank."

"You mean mink?"

"Yes," said the otter. "Mink came to my riverbank and simply took over the place. I moved down here to the sea for a little peace and quiet. I'm a solitary kind of animal, I like my own company, you know. And when I do socialise, I like to choose my company. Now

78

you salmon, I have always found to be excellent company. I do appreciate a little chat with a salmon, you are such widely travelled, genteel fish. By the way, is that common little seal with you?" The seal had been circling around them at a safe distance, taking care not to surface for air at the same time as the otter.

"I'm afraid so," said Duff. "He was driven out of his nursery by men with guns. His mother was killed. He just kept following us."

"Men," exclaimed the otter with a shudder of revulsion. "Yes, that's another reason I've come here. There are no men. My new home is inaccessible to them. But what are you going to do with the seal?"

"I thought we might sneak away and leave him here when he's asleep," said Gaffer.

"No, shame on you Gaffer," said Bubble indignantly. "You can't do that. We're hoping to find some of his own kind and leave him with them."

"Won't that be a little dangerous for you?" asked the otter.

"Yes, it's impossible," Gaffer agreed.

"Actually, seals congregate on that flat rock over there at the headland when the tide uncovers it. They're not exactly the sort of company I would choose for myself but I don't mind letting that little fellow stay till they show up. They're sure to be about in the morning. He can join them then."

"That's very kind of you," said Gaffer, delighted to be relieved of responsibility for the baby seal. "I don't know how to thank you."

"That's all right," said the otter. "I'm glad to do a good turn for old friends . . . that is, I think you're my old friends, but you know how it is, one salmon looks much like another."

They had trouble persuading the seal to stay with the otter. "He looks cross," protested the seal, "he told me to scram. I want to stay with you." He nuzzled Gaffer again. "You really do smell delicious." Gaffer retreated indignantly out of his reach.

"Other seals will come in the morning and you can be with your own kind," Coral Bud assured him. "We must go on and find our river. Salmon and seals just can't live together. You would eat us some day."

"I promise I will never eat you, Coral Bud," said the baby seal. He followed the otter ashore and the salmon slipped quietly away, swimming fast to make up for lost time.

11

The River

Next day they found what they were looking for. At
first the sensation came over them imperceptibly. They
had swum all night through the dark ocean, lit only by
starlight which glimmered intermittently through the
still water surface. Towards morning, offshore breezes
ruffled the surface of the water and splintered the pale
light of daybreak. They heard the pounding of surf on
a sandy shore and once they glimpsed a gaudy surf-
board speeding inshore on the swell for one brief
moment before it was buried in broken surf and its
human rider pounded by the churning wave.

They were suddenly possessed by new energy, as if
they could swim on and on for ever. In the shadow of
a black headland of overhanging cliff they encountered
a channel of fresh water, a wide deep channel floating
on the brine. It was not like any other fresh water that
they had tasted on their journey. Duff was first to
realise what it was. He rushed upwards and rolled over
on the surface, then flung himself joyously into the air.
Rocky followed him and then Coral Bud.

"It's our river," Duff cried out in delight. "We're
home!"

Fingal watched and listened enviously. Then,
suddenly, he too felt an irresistible urge to leap and
splash. He flung himself in the air. "This is ridiculous,"

he yelled at Gaffer as he tumbled down and saw Gaffer launch himself into the air, followed by Bubble. Then Storm rolled himself over and he and Elvira leaped and splashed just as foolishly as the wild fish.

"I can't help it," Gaffer spluttered and made another lunge for the surface. Fingal felt he just had to do the same. Then he realised what it was. This was home. It was just as the eel had said, they would know when they found their river because it would be home. He felt a terrible joy which made him tremble all over.

They rushed forward, following the channel of fresh water. "Careful," Gaffer warned. "It would be a pity to be caught in a net now, when we are so close to home."

Elvira was the first to see the river. "Look," she cried, dropping back into the water after a giddy lunge in the air. "I see the river." They all leaped and splashed and looked. "See how it floats, all white, on the surface of the ocean," exclaimed Elvira, "I remember when we were in the fish hatchery, I used to see that whiteness floating in the mornings but back then I didn't know what it was."

"No, that's not the river," Duff laughed. "That's the fog which lies on the river in the morning. It drifts out to sea and floats above the fresh water channels. You'll soon see the river underneath the fog."

Fingal remembered too. When he was very young and very small, in the tank in the hatchery, he had seen the white river fog lying above their tank in the mornings, but, like Elvira, he did not have a name for it. It was so easy now, to remember the taste of his river. The men had pumped the river water into the fish tanks and out again into the river. It was the sound they had heard continuously there, the sound of flowing river water, entering through filters into their tanks and flowing away again through a grid in the bottom. Now he tasted it again and leaped high to see the bank of river fog ahead. This was home.

"Careful," Gaffer called again and turned away from the fresh water channel. A wide net was stretched across their path. They swam cautiously around it. The rocky shoreline gave way to shingle which in turn gave way to sand.

They heard a sound so distant, so remote in memory that Fingal wondered if he had dreamed about it. As they drew closer to it he realised what it was. It was the rhythm of their own river bar, the river was singing its own song and the great surf crashing on the bar beat like a drum. They followed its music now as if mesmerised. All around them they sensed other fish also swimming towards the river. At last, where the river met the sea, they paused in a shallow inlet and found themselves among a large number of salmon, all waiting for the turn of the tide which would be the signal to enter the river.

"Fingal," said one of them, a large silver fish, almost as big as Gaffer, "is it really you?"

Fingal looked around him in disbelief. He recognised one fish, then another and then others who had been in the cage with him. So his group were not the only farm salmon to find their way to the river.

"Look at this, Gaffer," he exclaimed delightedly, "look, there are lots of us." The little inlet was crowded with fish who had escaped from the fish farm.

Gaffer, Bubble, Elvira and Storm swam about excitedly, greeting old friends. They introduced the farm fish to the three wild fish, Rocky, Duff and Coral Bud who were astonished to see so many very large salmon together in one place.

Then, they all became aware of a tremendous turbulence in the water. The force of the river current, which had seemed to overwhelm the power of the ocean, now weakened and yielded to the rush of the flooding tide. It was the signal the fish had been waiting for. "Let's go," said Gaffer. He turned and plunged forward through the churning waters. All of the salmon followed his lead, swimming eagerly into the river.

12

Willie's Story

On a green hill, overlooking the estuary and its morning blanket of fog, stood a small whitewashed house with a neat thatch of yellow rye straw tied down securely against winter storms. Inside, Willie was already up and stirring when the sun rose in the hills behind the small grey town further up the river. He moved stiffly about his kitchen. A black and white cattle dog, grown grey about the muzzle, followed the old man's movements with his eyes, waiting for the bowl of bread and sweet milky tea which was his breakfast.

"Here, Bran," said Willie, setting the bowl on the flagstone floor. The old dog lifted himself stiffly off the folded sacking that was his bed and sank his nose into the bowl. Willie poured the remaining tea into a flask and put it in a bag along with some bread and butter, wrapped in the greaseproof paper in which the loaf had come. Then he drew his waders on over knitted woollen socks. He left his bright yellow waterproof dopper on its peg beside the door. He would not need it today. A morning fog on the river channel was a sign of a fine day ahead.

When he was ready, he whistled to the dog who followed him, moving quietly, without excitement, carrying his head and tail low in the manner of a wise cattle dog. The road to the estuary wound downhill between high dry stone walls.

There were only four boats fishing the river estuary channel this season and as yet, only Willie's had cleared the cost of its fishing licence. The first catches of each boat went to clear the licence. Only after that was paid did anyone receive a share, one share for each crewman and one share for the owner of the boat and net.

The fishing was poor so far, and prices were low. The fish dealers said that the low cost of farmed salmon had knocked the bottom out of the price of wild salmon. Willie had nothing against fish farming. There was a salmon hatchery on up the river, above the town, where they bred young smolts for the fish farms in the sea. They re-stocked the river too, setting thousands of smolt free in the river each springtime. Eventually the restocking would restore the river's salmon run which had dwindled over the years because of pollution and fish disease.

If anyone had told him fifty years ago, Willie mused, that you could farm the river and the sea and rear fish the way livestock were reared on land he wouldn't have believed it. Still, that was progress. He had seen a lot of progress in his time, some good, some bad. Maybe he would see a good salmon run in the river again sometime. The fish might come back some day and he'd like to live to see that.

He could remember the time when a hundred boats and more fished the channel and fish were counted by the score, not in ones and twos. He was there seventy years ago when the fishermen fought the fisheries company for the right to fish. There weren't many who remembered that. He was a small boy that day, sent to his father's boat with a can of tea for the crew. He saw the fishery company's big motor launch ram the small fishing boats and toss their crews into the river. He stood and watched when the fishermen boarded the motor launch to retaliate. The dispute went to court but that was only the beginning of the story. The jurisdiction of the newly founded Free State was challenged by the fisheries company who rejected the decision of the Irish courts and appealed to the British House of Lords. The fight for the salmon fishing rights somehow became the fight of a small nation against an imperial power. The company lost its case and the fishermen won not only their right to fish but the right of their young nation state to its own independent courts.

Willie had told the story to the younger generation, to his nieces and nephews and to their children. Historians had visited him and recorded his eye-witness account of how the fishermen made history. But now, there was a generation who neglected the fishing. It looked as if their lack of interest might lose them the fishing right which had been so hard won.

Only yesterday evening his nephew Joe, a fine strong oarsman, had said he would not fish any more this season because his grass was ready for silage making. Willie's other nephew Dan had made an excuse too. He owned a turf cutting machine and cut turf on contract in the mountain bogs. "The lads will give you a hand," he promised, "when they get their holidays from school."

That's all salmon fishing meant to the next generation, Willie thought morosely, a pastime for old men and boys. He would have only two crewmen this morning, Dinny and James. They were almost as old as himself and growing soft, the pair of them. Dinny would be sure to have pains this morning and James might be hung over from his Sunday drinking. James would want a quiet easy job on the inside oar. Dinny would say he was too stiff with his rheumatism to row and would want to do budd.

The trouble was that he wasn't any good at doing budd. He wasn't watchful enough. The budd's job was to walk along the shore, holding the back rope and the sole rope as the boat towed the net downstream. It was his job as well to watch for any stir on the water surface, any flash of silver which would indicate a salmon moving upstream. A good budd gripped the ropes just firmly enough to hold them securely and just loosely enough to feel the touch of a fish against the net. Willie had been the best budd on the channel for many years now. He could see the flash of silver salmon far down-stream and could time the approach of the fish to the net. He would have his crew alert and ready for the split-second timing of the command "Go on." Then the outside oars would lunge in the water as the boat swept to the shore, the salmon, encircled by the net, thrashing and heaving.

He reached the level green where his net was spread to dry during the closed fishing period at the weekend. There was no sign of Dinny or James. He gathered up the net carefully and hoisted it on his back. Then he set off slowly through the fog to where his boat lay on its side on the wet estuary sand, beached by the falling tide. He boarded the net and waited.

The tide receded, baring wide stretches of sand and mud, dotted with the spiral casts of lugworms. If he waited much longer the tide would recede too far from the boat. It was just like Dinny and James to be late. They played cards with the neighbours half the night

and weren't fit to get out of bed in the morning.
Growing impatient, Willie went down to a crew of
three men who had already put their boat in the water
and were loitering on the shore. The other two licensed
boats were still up on the shore and it did not look as
if they would fish today.

"Maybe you lads would lend me a hand to put my
boat in the water?" he asked.

"You're getting too old to shift her yourself, eh
Willie?" said one of them. He was a tall, thick-set
young man, the owner of the boat and net. "Isn't it
time you packed in this game, Willie? You're getting
past it." He tossed the butt of a cigarette, which he had
been smoking, into the water, then pushed his boat
forward into deeper water, ready for boarding. "Come
on, boys, we'll shoot the net," he ordered his crew and
then turning back to Willie he said, "You'll not be
taking the first shot, after all, will you?" With a
mocking laugh he leapt into his boat.

"Sure, it'll only take a minute," protested one of his
crew, "he'll lose the whole tide if we don't put his
boat in the water now."

"If you want to fish with him, go ahead," said the
owner, "but if you want to stay on this crew you'd
better get into the boat."

Willie turned away. It was his turn today for first shot
on the flooding of the tide. The first shot of the tide
was always the best shot and the boats took it in turn.
Now, he would lose his shot. However, he knew better
than to argue about fishing. Fishing was a matter of
luck as well as skill and ill words or anger on the shore
had been known to turn away good luck for a whole
season. Willie had lived long enough to have seen such
things happen.

The man who took his shot he knew to be an ignorant stupid man with more greed for fish than knowledge of fishing. A week ago he had caught a seal and her pup in his net. The frantic animals tore the net in their struggle to escape. Enraged, the owner of the net attacked the mother seal with the butt of an oar but was driven back by her snapping jaws. She escaped into the river so he turned on the pup.

Willie saw what the man was doing and left his boat to go and stop him. "There were seals here before there were men and there will be seals after us," he said, appalled at the senseless brutality. "Let the pup alone."

"Are you going to stop me?" asked the man in an ugly tone turning menacingly towards Willie.

"I will if I have to," Willie said gravely and stood his ground. The younger man turned away and went back, still cursing, to his boat. Like a lot of bullies, he was brave just so long as nobody challenged him.

Willie examined the pup to see if it could be saved. It was beaten to a bloody pulp but still whimpered heart-rendingly. He took a piece of timber from his boat and struck the pup on the back of the head, killing it with a single blow. He wished he could have intervened in time to save it. It was wrong to take any young creature from its mother.

Since then, that man's boat had not seen so much as the tail of a salmon nor were they likely to. Bad luck always followed any person who did evil.

As the tide dropped, the river fog cleared and the morning sun shone brightly. Willie tired of waiting for Dinny and James. He walked, with Bran trotting at his heels, to the limit pole which marked the end of the permitted net fishing area and back again towards the bight pole, a hundred yards upstream. It was at this point or below that the first shot would be taken. Already, upstream, the boat was towing. They had a lazy, foolish way of fishing, without a budd, letting their ropes drag behind them.

Willie stood and gazed for a long time down the estuary. It was splendid in the light of late morning, a vast arena of clean yellow sand, closed on the south by steep, wind-sculpted sand dunes and on the north by a bank of limestone boulders. At its western end, where the river met the sea, surf pounded rhythmically on the sandbar. The air was filled with the incessant song of innumerable larks, hovering so high that they were mere specks in the sky. Willie felt the uplifting of the spirit that a beautiful day on the channel always gave him. The barely perceptible movement of water edging round his feet drew him back to earth. The tide had started to flood.

Automatically he looked down the river, scanning the surface for movement, for a tell-tale flash of silver. And then it came. Not one fish, but several, leaping with the excitement of journeying into their own river. They passed the limit pole, only a hundred yards below the fishing boat. Every instinct in Willie strained. If it had been any other boat he would have called out to alert them. The black and white dog looked at Willie and knew, from his years of following him to the channel, that fish were on their way. He too strained, tense and alert.

The salmon came closer and closer. It was impossible that the men in the boat did not see. One of the salmon, a twelve pound fish, at least half the length of a man, leaped and splashed joyfully. A man in the boat stirred and flicked cigarette ash in the water. The dog looked enquiringly at Willie, waiting expectantly for the drama and the excitement of the kill that would follow the command "Go on."

"Easy Bran, easy," Willie said, reaching down to touch him behind his ears, "let them go." Beside him, just a few yards away, a fish leapt, then another and another, all big fish. A score of salmon, maybe two score, maybe three. Willie's heart sang with happiness. He had lived to see the salmon run return to the river. The scores of big salmon were back, like in the old days.

He patted the dog and straightened up. "They'll be here after us, all right, and thank God I've lived to see it," he murmured quietly to himself.

Upstream, above the bight pole the boat was still towing. "Go on," shouted one of the men, aroused by the sound of a splash off their bow. The crew surged into action and the boat swept to the shore. They leapt out and seized the ropes which had been dragging behind. They were too late. Willie stood and watched as they hauled an empty net.

With a grim smile he turned away. It would be discourteous to gloat too much over an enemy. Far up the shore, two moving figures caught his eye. Dinny and James were hurrying across the sand. The old dog went towards them, wagging his tail in recognition. Willie waited till they drew close. "Well," he greeted them with mock indignation, "you could trawl hell with a herring net and not bring up two lazier blaggards than the pair of you."

"We would have been here sooner, only the old clock stopped," Dinny excused himself. "What time of day is it anyway?"

"Time for a cup of tea," Willie answered and reached into his boat for his flask and sandwiches. Dinny and

James settled themselves comfortably on the sand which had been dried by the hot sun. Willie poured a mug of tea for each of them and one for himself.

"Any fish got?" asked Dinny, biting into a piece of bread and butter.

"Not as much as a tail," replied Willie as he offered a piece of his bread to the old dog.

13

Death in the River

Gaffer had seen the draught net quite easily and led the group of fish aside from it, into the deep channel in the centre of the river. They were a very large group, made up of the farm fish and wild fish who had joined them outside the estuary. They swam eagerly upstream. The river channel wound across a wide sandy bed. The water tasted brackish, half salt and half fresh.

A mile or so upstream the sandy estuary channel widened into a rocky harbour basin with an island in its centre. Close to an old quay wall, the water was shaded by the dense green of trees. The salmon paused. They had reached their river now but the tidal water was still low. They could take time to amuse themselves here. Above them, on the shining surface, a dragonfly danced lightly. Fingal chased after it, giddy with the excitement of swimming in almost fresh water.

"Look out!" Duff yelled and rushed to head him off. "Don't you see that hook?"

Fingal stopped and looked. He saw that on the underside of the feathery dancing fly was a shining metal barb. "That's a hook?" he asked, horrified at the vicious looking object.

"Yes, it was with one just like it that I was caught," Duff warned. "Beware of pretty flies. Always look carefully for the hook. Man is very cunning. Look how it dances, just like a real fly."

Suddenly the shady quayside seemed full of menace. "Let's get out of here," Fingal urged Gaffer who was deep in conversation with one of their new friends, a hen salmon.

"He doesn't hear you," said Bubble. "Can't you see, he's busy. Not that I mind. There are plenty of fish in the sea, or in the river for that matter." She sounded vexed.

"Gaffer, let's go," Fingal insisted, "there's a man with a hooked fly fishing here."

"Did you say a hook?" Gaffer asked when he finally noticed that he was being spoken to by someone other than his new friend. "Where?"

Fingal showed him the dancing dragonfly. "My goodness, what a silly looking fly," said the hen salmon. She darted skittishly to the surface and snatched it in her mouth.

"No, stop," Fingal cried but he was too late.

"What is it?" screamed the hooked fish, thrashing against the pressure of the fisherman's line and leaping high above the surface. She dived and swam off in panic.

Duff swam after her. "Pull the line tight," he urged her but the man on the shore knew how to fish and fed out line as she dashed away. Despairing of escape, she turned and the other fish heard the click of the man's fishing reel as he reeled in his line. She felt once more the tug of the hook in her mouth and flung herself about in frenzy. "Swim away," Duff told her. "Swim as fast and as far as you can." She threw herself backwards along the surface. Once again the angler let her run with the line. Time was on his side. He needed only to play his fish and wait.

Fingal watched, sick with dread at what must follow.
The hooked fish dived among the weed-covered rocks
below and cowered there, quivering all over, from head
to tail. After what seemed an interminable delay she
broke again for open water. The man gave her line. She
surfaced once more and tried to snap the line with a
backward jerk. The man was ready and raised his rod to
take the strain. He was cunning, Fingal realised,
cunning as the devil himself who is the spirit of evil in
man.

They watched, appalled, as the gruesome ritual
unfolded. The salmon's mouth was bleeding. She was
growing weaker, exhausted by pain and the fight for
survival, but still she broke for freedom again and
again, only to be given line, then held, then given line
again, till at last the angler knew it was time to reel her
in. He reeled cautiously, ready to give way if she
should find some new, unexpected surge of strength.
Finally he drew her close to the riverbank, scooped her
into a net and it was all over.

Bubble swam close to Gaffer and nudged him gently.
"I'm glad you were nice to her," she said quietly.
Gaffer didn't reply. "Let's go away from here," Bubble
urged him, "the tide is rising. It's time to go."

"Yes," said Gaffer finally, "you're right, Bubble. Let's
go." He turned and headed upstream, followed by the
other salmon. They swam doggedly into the river
current which flowed strongly against the flooding tide.

Upstream, they reached a weir where the water
churned and frothed. One by one they leaped upwards
to the calm stream above. The excitement of leaping
restored their spirits a little.

The river had narrowed now and flowed rapidly
between high smooth walls. Rocky and Storm swam

close behind Gaffer and behind them swam Fingal and Coral Bud. Elvira and Duff were alongside. Although they had been joined by so many others, they were inclined to keep to their own group.

"This part of the river has been caged in by men. This fast flowing channel is called the tail-race, and those arches upstream are a bridge where men cross the river," explained Rocky, who had been this way before.

"You will see many bridges," said Duff, "men put them over the river wherever they want to cross it." They passed under the arches of the bridge. Ahead of them loomed a huge high wall.

Gaffer hesitated, and turned to ask Rocky, "What's that? Where does the river go?"

"That's the dam," she replied, "it was built by men to harness the power of the river."

"But how do we get round it?" Gaffer asked. He could see no way through.

"There's a fish-pass, on the left side of the river. We'll come to it soon," Duff assured him, swimming forward to show the way.

Gaffer and the other fish followed but Fingal felt a peculiar longing to turn right. "Where are you going? That's not the way," Elvira scolded him, when he turned aside. He turned back once more to follow the others but felt an indescribable urge to turn right again.

"I want to go that way," he said. "I don't know why."

Gaffer hesitated and turned back to Fingal. "You want to go that way too?" he asked.

"Yes," Fingal agreed, "I think home is that way."

Duff swam back to them impatiently. "You can't go that way. The fish-pass is on the other side. There is only one way to pass the dam."

"He's right," Rocky agreed and the other wild fish who had passed that way before murmured in assent.

"I want to go that way. I just want to," Fingal insisted.

"I know how you feel," Gaffer said sympathetically. "I feel just the same."

"So do I," said Elvira.

"Me too," agreed Storm. All the farm fish looked at each other and agreed. They wanted to go the other way.

"Let's check it out," said Gaffer, swimming forward to follow the tiny eddy of current which seemed so terribly attractive to all the farm fish.

"There's nothing there except the spillway," insisted Duff. "You can't swim up that."

Gaffer nosed about near the edge and found what he was looking for, a pipe, protruding from the riverbank. The enticing flow of water, which had drawn him here, was issuing from it. It didn't make sense. The pipe was not wide enough to let a salmon pass. Puzzled, he pushed his head in to see if he could find an answer to the mystery.

"Don't do that, Gaffer," Fingal warned. He was afraid of a trap. He remembered the old salmon who had moralized about the tinker who became a salmon. Don't put your head into anything you can't get it out of, he had warned. However, Gaffer reversed from the pipe without difficulty.

"What is it?" he asked in bewilderment. All the farm fish crowded round the pipe. They felt a ridiculous urge to go into it. Then it dawned on Fingal what it was. The water in the pipe tasted of the big blue tanks in the fish hatchery. It tasted of the fishmeal which they had eaten when they were small fry.

"It's the hatchery!" he exclaimed in delight. "We really are home." He was so pleased with his discovery that he leapt clear of the water. When he was in mid-air he saw the blue fish-hatchery tanks, line after line of them, ranged on a green hillside beside the river.

The farm fish leapt to look and hooted and jeered in delight.

"We may be home," said Gaffer, "but we're not going to stay. Come on Duff, show us the way."

The dam was an exciting place with a mighty cascade of water tumbling from the sluice gates at the top, down the spillway and into the tail-race below. The salmon paused to play in the churning water, leaping wildly to see which fish could go farthest up the rushing stream. When they were exhausted, they lay in the calm pool behind the spillway wall and rested. Night fell but instead of stars shining dimly through the surface, the water was brilliantly illuminated by lights which shone from the high dam wall and from the bridge downstream.

Suddenly, they noticed that the pool was filled with a dense mass of tiny, squirming transparent fish, each one glowing with phosphorescence. Fingal looked closely at them. One tiny fish detached itself from the wriggling mass, approached Fingal and looked equally closely at him. "What are you?" Fingal asked.

"What's it to you?" the small fish said cheekily and then turned and wriggled away, indistinguishable from the millions of other small fish in the pool.

"They're elvers, that is, young eels," said one of the wild salmon. "They always appear in the river unexpectedly like this."

"That's right," explained an elderly wild salmon, "Eels don't spawn like other fish. They just appear. I always heard it said that they are spawned out of the dew that falls on the river at this time of year."

Fingal didn't wish to offend the old salmon by appearing to know more than him so he did not tell him how the eel elvers travelled from the Sargasso sea.

Elvira, however, was not so discreet. "What a silly notion," she hooted, "how could you be so silly as to believe that a fish is spawned out of dew? Eels are spawned in the Sargasso sea." She addressed herself to the squirming mass. "Isn't that so?" she said.

A small eel detached himself once again. Fingal could not be certain it was the same one who had spoken to him. "That's none of your business," the elver snapped at Elvira and disappeared into the crowd at once so that she could not tell which of them had been rude to her.

"Well, I don't think much of their manners," she said indignantly.

"Their manners aren't any worse than yours," said the old salmon severely to Elvira.

Suddenly the dense, wriggling, shining mass of eels disappeared as unexpectedly as it had appeared.

"Where have they gone?" Elvira asked.

"They've gone to their own fish-pass," said the old salmon. "It's much smaller and narrower than ours but they seem to manage."

"Oh," said Elvira, a little deflated to find that the old salmon could teach her something after all.

Fingal noticed a larger, full grown eel stir from a crevice in the spillway wall and approach the salmon. It was a peculiar looking eel with an flat funnel shaped mouth. "Lamprey," shouted the old salmon, and swam quickly away.

"What?" said Fingal looking about for danger but only seeing only the odd looking eel. "Ouch!" he screamed as it lunged forward and attached itself to his underside. He dashed himself against the spillway wall to try to detach the horrible thing. It gripped tighter with the sucker which was its mouth and sank its teeth into his flesh. The pain was excruciating. Fingal cried out in terror.

"What is it?" Duff swam up to him and he and Elvira looked in horror at the lamprey eel which had attached itself to Fingal. They swam at it and tried to butt the disgusting parasite away from Fingal's body but it simply clung more tightly. Fingal flung himself at the spillway wall once more, dragging his body along it, in an effort to dislodge the lamprey.

Coral Bud came to help. She swam alongside Fingal, urging him to try harder.

Rocky joined the group of onlookers. She spoke in a quiet voice so that Fingal would not hear. "There's nothing we can do. The lamprey will feed on him till he's too weak to survive. We had better move on. There may be more lampreys here. They lie in wait in estuary waters to attach themselves to migrating fish."

Gaffer came and circled round Fingal anxiously. He smashed his tail against the lamprey but his huge strength had no effect. The lamprey's sucker seemed immovable. "Can you swim straight?" he finally asked. They would try to keep Fingal with them as long as possible.

Fingal stopped trying to shake off the lamprey, steadied himself and tried to swim in a straight line. It was awkward and painful with the lamprey attached but he found he could still swim forward.

"You lead us up the fish-pass," Gaffer said to Duff. "I'll swim with Fingal."

They made their way into the fish-pass. The fish-pass

consisted of a series of long, narrow, man-made pools, each one higher than the previous one. The river water was channelled through the pass and by leaping from one trough of water to the next one above it, the fish could climb the steep side of the dam. For Fingal, hampered by the weight of the lamprey and weakened by pain and shock, it was an ordeal.

"Jump, Fingal, jump," Gaffer urged at the end of each pool when they had to leap to a higher stage.

"Please, Fingal, you must get up," Coral Bud pleaded. She had stayed behind with Fingal because she could not bear to go on without him. The other fish were far ahead.

Fingal struggled onwards. It seemed pointless to keep leaping up and up. He would never be able to detach the lamprey from his body. It would destroy him long before he would ever reach the spawning beds.

"Jump, Fingal," Gaffer urged him when he wanted to rest.

"I can't, it hurts too much," Fingal moaned.

"You can rest in the next pool," Coral Bud coaxed him.

He braced himself and leaped. The lamprey seemed enormously heavy. The leap was not high enough. His body struck painfully off the wall of the fish-pass and he fell back into the lower pool.

"Try again," urged Gaffer, "don't give up."

He leaped again and this time splashed into the pool above. Coral Bud and Gaffer splashed into the pool alongside him. He noticed dimly that the series of stepped troughs gave way now to a long conduit of water which appeared to pass right into one of the brightly lit buildings beside the dam. It was easier to swim there. Fingal followed Gaffer and Coral Bud into the bright flood of light.

"Men!" Gaffer called out in alarm and leaped in an attempt to turn round in the pass but the passage behind was slammed closed. They had swum into a trap. A man stood ready with a net.

"Here's a fine big fellow, will I fish him out?" he asked.

They heard another man reply, "No, we have enough cock salmon for now. Are there any hen fish?" Coral Bud tried to cringe out of sight. The first man reached with the net and scooped her into it.

"She's a bit small, her first season, I'd say," he said, holding her in the net without taking her out of the water.

The second man appeared and looked down at Coral Bud. Fingal and Gaffer recognised him. He was the man from the hatchery who had come each day with the thermometer.

"No, she's a bit small. We'll leave her till next year," he said, "turn her loose." He noticed Fingal and peered down into the water. "There's a fish in trouble," he said, "he's got a lamprey underneath. Here, give me the net."

He slipped the net off Coral Bud and Fingal found himself suddenly lifted from the water, suspended in the net. "Let those other two fish go on ahead," the man said to his assistant.

He laid Fingal on a table and slipped the net off him. He was a tall, sturdy man with strong, careful hands. He seized the lamprey with one hand, held Fingal firmly with the other and pulled the parasite away from his body. He flung the lamprey into a large bin beside the table and then gently placed the salmon in a large tank of water. "We'll leave him there for a while till he recovers from the shock," he said. "That's a nasty lesion, but I think we've got him in time."

Fingal realised he was a prisoner in the tank but still, the relief was enormous. The lamprey was gone and even though it had left a large painful sore on his underside he was certain that he would survive. The man had let Gaffer and Coral Bud continue on their way. Whatever his reason for trapping them, it was not to kill them.

14

A Science Project

On the far side of the street which ran parallel to the
river on its northern side was an old stone wall, which
surrounded a yellow pebble-dashed building and a
huddle of prefabricated classrooms. There was also a
basketball court and several lawns where cherry trees in
bloom scattered pink blossoms on the grass. Inside the
building, Shawn and Ashling, both second year students,
stood in the vice-principal's office.

"Humph," said the vice-principal, looking at them
severely over the top of his spectacles, "you want
permission to be absent from class to visit this . . . er . . .
this fish hatchery?"

"Yes sir, it's for our science project," Shawn explained.

"And for how long do you expect to be absent?"
asked the vice-principal.

"We're not sure," said Ashling. "The man didn't say
how long it would take."

"Humph," said the vice-principal again. "Well, make
sure you're back in time for the first class after lunch."

They hurried outside, checked Shawn's bicycle bag
again to make sure he had their note-books and camera
safe inside, then jumped on to their bicycles and sped
out through the school gate. A passing lorry honked
loudly. "Look out where you're going," the driver
shouted. Shawn made a rude sign with his fingers and
cycled away as fast as he could.

Ashling followed. "You'll get us into trouble," she said in a shocked voice.

Shawn looked back over his shoulder. The lorry was a long way behind, held up by traffic in the narrow street. "Nah, he's miles behind," he said cheerfully and swerved round the corner into the next street.

He had chosen salmon as his topic for his science project because it was a really interesting topic. He already knew a lot about salmon from listening to his father and his father's uncle Willie. Uncle Willie was the best salmon fisherman on the channel. Shawn was looking forward to fishing on his crew as soon as he got his summer holidays in a fortnight's time. Then he would be a real fisherman.

It was Ashling's idea to visit the fish hatchery. She'd chosen salmon as her project because she couldn't bear earthworms and the thought of liver fluke made her feel ill. The life cycles of the earth worm and the liver fluke were the other topics on offer for their science projects. She had telephoned the fish hatchery and asked for permission to see the fish. Shawn approved of that. Anything was better than being in class on a beautiful sunny day like this.

The man in the fish hatchery was expecting them. "You're just in time. We only strip a small number of June fish. We hold most of the breeding stock till autumn. But we've a pair here for you to see." He showed them two salmon in the holding tank. "You can see that these salmon are ready for mating. Look how they've turned red around the gills. Once a salmon comes into the river it begins to assume its mating colours."

Shawn sniggered and nudged Ashling. She glared at him and he tried to look serious.

106

The man went on talking. He took the hen salmon from the holding tank and, pressing gently on her sides, he expressed her eggs into a bowl. "What I am doing now is called stripping the salmon. That means taking away the eggs and the milt. These are unfertilised ova." He put the hen salmon back into the tank and carefully lifted out a cock salmon in the net. "Now, I'll do the same thing with the male fish," he explained. He stroked the sides of the male fish just as he had done with the female. "This is the milt which is the sperm of the male fish. The milt contains millions of minute spermatozoa. One will enter each egg and fertilize it, when we mix them in the bowl."

Ashling took several photographs of the stripping of the eggs and the milt. She and Shawn watched, fascinated, as they were mixed in the bowl and wrote the names of everything in their notebooks. "Will they hatch into salmon now?" Ashling asked.

"Yes, the time will depend on the temperature of the water. In arctic regions the incubation period is much longer than here. We measure the incubation in degree days. This is a calculation which takes temperature into account. The salmon hatches in five hundred and ten degree days. Now, have you got all that written down?"

"Oh yes, this is brilliant," said Shawn, as it dawned on him that he was witnessing the miracle of spawning, a sight that none of the salmon fisherman he knew had ever seen. When he was part of Uncle Willie's salmon fishing crew he would be able to tell how he had seen salmon eggs being fertilized in the hatchery. Not even Uncle Willie had seen that.

"Would you like to see the young fish now?" the man asked.

"Yes, please," they replied eagerly.

The man led them to the hatchery tanks where tiny fry swam about, looking ridiculously small in the enormous blue tanks. "When they weigh about fifty grams they turn silver and we call them smolts. It takes about a year. Then they're ready for the sea. We sent all of this year's smolts to the sea in April. Did you see the helicopters carrying them?"

"Yes, I did," said Ashling. "I took photographs of them."

"Good," said the man, "now, have you any questions?"

"What happens to the big fish, now that you have taken away their eggs and their milt?" Shawn asked.

"We put them back in the river. You can stay and see it if you like."

Ashling looked at her watch. They still had half an hour to spare before first class after lunch. "Yes, we'd like to see that," she said. They followed the man back into the building where they had seen the stripping of the salmon.

The hen and cock salmon were still in the holding tank. The man netted each of them in turn and put them into the fish-pass. "They'll go back to the sea now that they've spawned," he explained.

"What about this one here," Ashling enquired about a large salmon in another tank. "Is he ready to go back to the sea?"

"No, he's recovering from an attack by a lamprey. We fished him out of the pass last night."

"What's a lamprey?" Ashling asked.

"It's a parasitical creature which attaches itself to fish and feeds on them. Look, it's still there in the bin. You can see the mark on the salmon's underbelly where the lamprey attached itself to him."

"Yeuch," said Ashling when she saw the hideous, sucker shaped mouth of the dead lamprey.

Shawn looked at it curiously. "A lamprey once tried to attach itself to my great Uncle Willie's wader, when he was fishing on the channel. He had to beat it off with a stick."

"I can believe that," said the man, "they're very tenacious creatures. Now, I think this salmon is ready for the river again. He hasn't mated yet so he'll travel on up-river for another while." The man reached into the tank and scooped Fingal into the net. He placed him carefully in the fish-pass and released him from the net. Fingal shivered all over with delight to find himself in the flow of river water again. With a powerful lash of his tail, he lunged forward and leaped upward on the next stage of his climb up the fish-pass.

"Any more questions?" asked the man.

"I wonder," Ashling asked tentatively, "I wonder if you can tell me how I can become a fish farmer. I used to want to be a nurse but I think I've just changed my mind."

15

Searching

When Fingal emerged from the fish-pass he found himself in a wide, island-dotted lake. The water was murky and brown, quite unlike the river water below the dam which was slightly salty from the tidal waters which invaded it twice a day. The raw wound on his underbelly where the lamprey had attacked him still ached, but had already begun to heal. Fingal followed the main channel in the deepest part of the lake where a strong current flowed. The current would lead him in the direction that his friends had taken.

A large coarse-scaled fish swam near to him. His appearance reminded Fingal of the ballan wrasse which he had met in the sea. His markings and coarse scales were similar but his head and mouth were quite different. The fish stopped, curious to find itself observed by a salmon. "Hi, salmon," it said, "can I help you?"

"Did you see any salmon pass this way last night?" asked Fingal.

"Salmon pass this way all the time at this season. Follow the channel and you'll catch up with them," said the fish.

"Thanks," said Fingal, "by the way, what kind fish are you? Excuse my asking, I'm new here."

"I'm a perch," the fish replied. "I live here all the time."

"A perch," echoed Fingal. He remembered the trout's story of the river fish, and their names, the perch, the pike, the bream, the roach. He felt a thrill of excitement that he was now in the trout's fresh water domain where these fabled creatures lived.

Over the days which followed he met all of them. He saw a long slender pike with his ferocious flattened head and narrow, slitted eyes lurking in reeds near a small island, ready to pounce on any smaller fish which passed that way. He met perch frequently. They were talkative, inquisitive fish, just like the ballan wrasse, only not at all timid. They wanted to hear the news and gossip which he might have gleaned on his journey up the great lake and were quite irritated with him for being in such a hurry to press onward. He saw large solitary bream grubbing for worms in the muddy shallows and shoals of roach flitting among the islands, totally absorbed in their own affairs and ignoring the passing salmon. There were trout too, brown, fresh water trout who had never travelled further from the lake than to some small tributary stream in spawning season.

All of them had seen salmon but none of them could give much detail about the salmon they had seen.

"You know how it is," an otter explained, swimming in graceful circles round Fingal when he stopped near its holt to make enquiries, "one salmon is much like another." Fingal had a feeling he had had this conversation somewhere before. The otter looked exactly like the otter whom Fingal and his friends had met in the sea, who had taken the baby seal into his care. One otter looks much like another too, he thought ruefully as he turned away and swam onward.

He had travelled for many days when the lake

narrowed to the width of its channel and became a
river again. The water grew dark and dirty and soon
the river passed between high, stone, man-made walls
and under the arches of many bridges.

Fingal swam quickly, hoping to escape the foul taste
which permeated the water. Everywhere there were
pipes discharging filthy effluents into the river. The
water stank of man and his uncleanliness. There were
bream and perch there, nosing about the pipes and
feeding on the putrid matter which emerged from
them. Fingal was appalled to think that fish could spend
their lives in such a place and hurried by without
asking them if they had seen his friends.

Soon he was upstream from the town which had
fouled the river and the water was pure and clean once
more. The river widened yet again into a vast expanse
of lake. Now Fingal was obliged to travel more slowly.
He could taste, in the lake, the waters of many tributary
rivers. His friends could have gone to any one of them.
He hoped they had all made the journey safely. As days
and weeks passed, and he still did not catch up with
them, he tried not to wonder if Coral Bud would have
taken up with somebody new.

In the first of the tributary rivers, a slow, sluggish
stream which meandered between densely growing
reeds, he asked a water hen, who was clucking fussily
over the immense task of escorting her brood of chicks,
if she had seen salmon. "Salmon?" she exclaimed
irritably, "for goodness sake, I don't have time to look
at every passerby. Can't you see I'm busy, come along
chicks, do smarten yourselves, come along."

Fingal then asked a very small trout who retreated in
panic into the reeds at the sight of such a large fish.
"Don't be afraid of me," said Fingal, "I'm a salmon.

We're brothers." The trout emerged cautiously, looking at him with round astonished eyes. "Haven't you ever seen a salmon before?" Fingal asked. The small trout, dumbfounded, shook his head. Fingal realised his friends couldn't be in this river and turned downstream again.

The next river which he investigated was a turbulent, brown stream, at times flowing rapidly over rocky shallows, at other times moving slowly through deep brown pools of bog water. He swam vigorously upstream, pausing to ask a small freshwater crayfish if he had seen salmon. The crayfish crawled quickly out of sight, under a stone, without answering him. Fingal paused in a deep pool which eddied darkly under the shade of an overhanging rock and wondered whether to continue upstream or turn back to the lake. His thoughts were interrupted by the voices of men.

He looked and saw them clearly through the brown mountain water. They were crouched under the overhang of the rock, which, on the riverbank, was almost a cave. Near them were several large round containers, and the men had made a fire, over which they had placed a smaller container. They were absorbed in their work and Fingal watched, intrigued. They did not seem to pose any threat or danger to him. He could see no sign of lures or hooks or nets. And besides, the men had their backs turned to the river. Whatever they were doing, it was not fishing.

"Easy now," said one of them, "seal the worm there at your end."

"Worm," Fingal echoed to himself. Of course he knew what a worm was. Trout ate them. Perhaps men did too.

One of the men stood up. "Did you hear something?" he asked.

The other man stood also, moved from the shelter of the rock and looked down the mountainside. "It's the law, they must know we're here," he exclaimed, "quick, get rid of this lot. Don't leave any evidence or we'll get six months jail."

They flung something into the pool. A long spiral-shaped metal pipe sank slowly to the bottom. Then the men tossed the containers on their sides and let them spill into the river. They turned and ran upstream along the riverbank, racing among the rocks that overhung the river. Some of the contents of the containers ran into Fingal's pool. The taste was strange but not unpleasant.

Several men, dressed in dark blue, appeared on the riverbank. They wore caps with shining silver badges. To Fingal, they all looked alike. They examined the empty containers and looked into the brown pool.

"It's illegal distilling, all right," said one.

"Poteen," said another. "We'll have to drag this pool with a grappling hook. They may have dumped their equipment into it." He peered into the depths of the pool searching for the tell-tale spiral shape of a copper condensation tube which, if they found it, would be an indisputable piece of evidence.

"Hey, take a look at this," exclaimed a third, "is that a salmon down there?"

They crowded together and looked. "Would you believe that," said one. "It's the first time I've heard of salmon in this river."

Fingal realised that once again he was in the wrong river. Somehow, he didn't really care. He knew he should have darted away when the men on the riverbank talked about him but he felt oddly carefree and excited. He felt a sudden urge to show off and flung himself up in the air in a flamboyant leap. The men gasped in astonishment. "I wouldn't have believed it if I hadn't seen it with my own eyes," exclaimed one.

"Incredible," said another.

"Look," said a man who was examining one of the empty containers, "they've emptied the wash into the river." He looked down at Fingal who was now giddily chasing his tail. "That salmon is going to have one heck of a party," he said sympathetically, "and tomorrow he'll have one terrible headache."

16

Fingal and the Gods

Fingal didn't notice when the men went away. He pursued his tail till he was dizzy. It then occurred to him that this was frivolous behaviour, unworthy of a salmon. He thrust his tail firmly behind him where he would no longer see it and feel impelled to pursue it. Then he steadied himself with great care and assumed the dignified, stately deportment proper to a salmon. It was time for the most noble of fish to review his kingdom.

The current carried him downstream, a proceeding which, he felt, was most appropriate for a fish of his importance. He nodded majestically to the left and right, at minnows and sticklebacks, and heaved his dorsal fin briefly to the surface in a stately acknowledgment of the adulation of numerous gnats which dropped their curtseys on the surface of the stream.

"I am a salmon, king among fish," he declared for the benefit of any creature who might not have realised that the noble fish, Fingal, was in their midst. The brown rushes which grew sparsely on the thin mountain soil bowed in the breeze as he passed, and Fingal acknowledged their obeisance with a gracious nod.

He continued his royal progress downstream, noticing, on his way, that the sun had set simultaneously in the north and the east and the west. Night fell and through the brown mountain water, he saw five moons rise in a starry sky. "I am the current in the mountain stream, I am the great waters of the earth, I am the universe," uttered Fingal, filled with the ineffable wisdom of transcendent salmonhood.

He swam on his side, slithering over little cataracts and through frothing rapids. He swam on his back, his white belly turned upwards, shining in the pale yellow light of five moons. Then a black shape rose before him. A long jagged rock jutted half-way across the stream.

"I am the rock that bars the stream," said the rock in a loud aggressive tone.

Fingal paused. He could swim round the rock, but it seemed to him that the rock's discourteous manner and its uncouth words were lacking in that deference which was due from a lowly rock to a noble salmon. "Stand aside," said Fingal.

"Stand aside yourself," said the rock, in a tone of calculated insult.

Fingal felt that this could only be read as a direct challenge, not merely to his own personal dignity, but to the dignity of all salmonkind. He accepted the challenge. With a powerful thrust of his tail, he lunged forward and butted the rock as hard as he could. "Take that," he said unsteadily as the current snatched him away and swept him downstream. "And show a little more respect next time you meet a salmon," he shouted although he was now too far away from the offending rock to be heard.

The stream flowed into the great, wide expanse of lake and Fingal floated belly-up, too drowsy now even to consider righting himself. He would have been quite happy to sleep like that had he not been aroused unexpectedly by a tall bullrush which insisted upon talking to him. "You there," said the bullrush.

Fingal thought it odd that a bullrush would commence a conversation in such an abrupt manner. However, as he considered how he should reply, he realised that this bullrush had addressed him in a singularly lofty, godlike manner and that he must reply with proper deference. "Who, me?" he answered drowsily.

"Yes, you."

Fingal dozed a little as he waited to hear what the bullrush would say next.

"Where's the party?" it asked in a god-like tone.

It dawned on Fingal that this was Manannan, the fun-loving god of the sea. "Party?" he yawned, "what party?"

"The party you were at," said Manannan. "You look as if you've been having a good time."

"Are you really Manannan?" asked Fingal.

Manannan turned himself into a large red and white buoy with a small blue flag on top and replied, "Yes, I am Manannan, God of the sea, and you are one of my subjects. Now, kindly tell me where the party is. I don't like to miss a party."

Fingal puzzled. "Party?" Dimly, he remembered. One of the men in blue, by the brown pool which tasted so strangely, had said that Fingal was going to have a party.

"Well?" said Manannan, metamorphosing into an empty beer can, and bobbing impatiently among the ripples on the surface of the lake, "where's the action?"

"Up the mountain river, in a brown pool, under a high rock," Fingal directed him.

Manannan disappeared. "Hey, come back," Fingal called. He wanted to ask him for directions to the spawning streams but Manannan did not hear.

"Can I help you?" asked a small brown water vole who had been observing Fingal with growing concern as he conversed first with a bullrush, then with a red and white buoy and finally with an empty beer can.

Fingal turned to see who had spoken. He saw a small animal with glossy black fur and a short rounded muzzle looking at him with acute black eyes. "I'm looking for Manannan, god of the sea," he explained. "He was here just a minute ago."

The vole considered the problem. "Manannan," he said, clasping and unclasping his pale pink forepaws, as he weighed the difficulties of the situation.

"Yes Manannan," said Fingal. "I need to ask him the way."

"A sea god, you say?"

"Yes, a sea god," Fingal agreed.

The vole tut-tutted sympathetically. Fish, at their best, were seldom lucid creatures, he knew, but this salmon was a worse case than most. The poor fish was obviously insane. His best policy, the vole decided, would be to humour the unfortunate creature. "I have heard that the gods live in the east, beyond the rising sun," he advised. "If you go that way, you are sure to catch up with er . . . what did you say his name was?"

"Manannan."

"Oh yes, of course, Manannan, a sea god, isn't that what you said? Yes, well, you just swim east and you'll find him." The vole had seen many salmon before, on their migrations through the lake. In this season they always travelled east. If Fingal would go towards the east he would follow the proper route for a salmon. Then the vole could alert other passing salmon to look out for him. Perhaps he would recover his wits in the company of his own kind.

"Which way is east?" Fingal knew that he should know which way was east but just now he couldn't work it out.

Oh dear, thought the vole, disorientated too. A bad case, certainly. To Fingal he said, "Go towards the sunrise," and he pointed to where the sky was already streaked with morning light.

Fingal turned and went towards the light. A golden path opened before him and all around him he heard the song of the river mingled with the song of the earth and the song of the sky. He passed beyond the burning light and then he was overwhelmed by a sense of awe and dread and hesitated to go any further. Three wooded islands appeared before him, merged and became one. Three swans descended from the sky with a loud clamour of wings and came to rest on the golden water. They reached their slender necks under the shimmering surface and became salmon. "Fingal," they asked in one voice, "why have you entered our domain?" As they spoke they merged into one gleaming salmon goddess and then parted again and became three.

Fingal tried to remember why he had wanted to swim beyond the rising sun. His body ached. He needed to rest. He wanted to find Gaffer and Silver Bud. "I have been trying to find my friends," he said.

"First, you must rest," said the Triple Goddess in a gentle voice, "then you will find your friends." The three islands which had been one became three again and clustered together to make a shallow bay, shaded by overhanging boughs of ancient oak trees. Fingal rested there, cradled in golden water, rocked in the arms of the goddess.

17

Found

He dreamed. There were voices in his dream, speaking from very far away. "Fingal, what's the matter with you?" said one.

"Do you think he's dead?" That was a voice which quivered, on the brink of grief.

"Never mind, Coral Bud," said a third voice. "There are lots of other handsome cock salmon around. You'll find someone else." That had to be Elvira.

"I don't want anyone else," said Coral Bud, stifling a sob.

Fingal stirred in his dream and answered them. "Motormouth," he said, "trust you, Elvira, to say the wrong thing."

"What did he say? Did you hear what he said?"

"No, I heard nothing."

"He said something. I know he said something."

"I said motormouth," Fingal repeated but they didn't seem to hear. He ached all over. His head felt as if he had been hitting it off a rock. It was midday, he knew, because he could feel the sun's heat penetrating the water of the shallow bay where he had been sleeping. How very odd, he thought, to be asleep in broad daylight. He remembered vaguely that he had gone to sleep in the shelter of a tree-covered island . . . or was it two tree-covered islands . . . or even three? That didn't make sense. He dismissed the memory. It must have been a dream. The warm water was stifling. No wonder that his head ached.

"Look at that bump on his head. You'd think he had been hit with a rock."

A rock, of course, there had been an altercation with an ill-mannered rock . . . no, that didn't make sense either. He must have dreamed that too. His body seemed an enormous weight. If he stirred a fin or moved his tail fractionally, he was overwhelmed with nausea. It reminded him of the day that pig slurry had been carried by the tide into his cage at the fish farm, only this time he felt much worse. "Poisoned," he thought, remembering the word the men had used that day. "I've been poisoned by something," he said to himself and he remembered the peculiar taste of the contents of the containers which had spilled into the brown pool in the mountain stream.

"Poisoned, he said poisoned," said one of the voices in his dream.

Manannan, he suddenly remembered, he had sent Manannan up there. Was it Manannan, the sea god, who had spoken with him? Could such a thing have happened? He searched his memory. Bit by bit the recollection came to him. Something else, something far more important had happened, something so serene and so beautiful that nothing in his life would ever again be equal to it. The memory eluded him. He remembered three wooded islands or was it only one? An image surfaced dimly in his mind of three swans . . . or was it three salmon . . . or was it only one? The images were confused. She, or they, had spoken to him. He remembered experiencing a moment of ineffable wonder. Had he, of all fish, seen the Triple Goddess of earth and ocean and sky? Was it she who had promised that he would find his friends? He dreamed their voices again.

"Fingal, wake up Fingal." It was Gaffer's voice this time.

"Fingal, don't die on me." That was Coral Bud.

The voices were close to him now. Slowly, it dawned on Fingal that he was not dreaming any more. His friends were really there. "Coral Bud," he said aloud and shook himself awake. "Ouch, my head," he gasped as the impact of his movement struck him.

"Oh Fingal, you're alive," exclaimed Coral Bud and she nuzzled him gently. "We had almost given up on you."

"What happened to you?" asked Duff, "you look terrible."

"I had an argument with a rock," said Fingal, looking at them all with delight but holding himself carefully, hardly daring to move. He felt as if he were made of something fragile which might break if he moved too suddenly.

"I take it you lost the argument?" said Elvira drily.

"It feels that way," Fingal agreed.

"We've been searching for you all morning," said Gaffer.

"How did you know I was here?"

"A water vole told us to watch out for an extremely crazy salmon," replied Gaffer, "we knew that could be nobody but you."

"But where have you been? What have you been doing?" Coral Bud asked.

Fingal turned and looked at her. Her silver fins shimmered in the noonday sunlight which quivered everywhere in the water. He dimly remembered another shimmering salmon which became three and then became one again.

"Are you all right?" asked Coral Bud. "Why are you looking at me like that?"

Fingal groped in his memory for an answer but the image in his mind faded. He saw Coral Bud and forgot the vision he had been trying to remember. "I'm so glad to see you again," he said. "I thought you would have forgotten about me."

"She has thought of nothing else, since we were in the fish-pass," exclaimed Bubble. "Doesn't he look handsome in his mating colours?" she added, turning to Coral Bud.

Fingal suddenly noticed that his friends no longer wore the silver sheen of sea fish. They had turned golden brown and their gills and throats were rose pink. "Have I changed my colours too?" he asked, startled to think it could have happened without his noticing.

"Yes you have," Coral Bud said shyly, "and your new colours suit you terribly well."

18

Slurry

Fingal recovered enough to swim with the others to deeper, cooler water. Coral Bud swam alongside him, watching solicitously to see that he was all right. He soon felt much better.

"Where are the others?" he asked when they had been swimming across the lake's deep channel for a while.

"Rocky tasted the waters of her spawning stream two days ago," Coral Bud replied. "We've been following its current through the lake since then. She and Storm went on ahead this morning to find it. The rest of the fish went with them. We stayed behind to search for you. Nobody really believed that we would find you. They thought you died, back at the fish-pass. We waited at the top of the pass till daybreak, then Gaffer said we would have to go on. I was afraid I would never see you again. When we met that funny little water vole this morning I knew he had to be talking about you."

Soon, they found the waters of Rocky's spawning stream, mingled with the water of the lake. "This way," Gaffer called out and led the way to the shore where the stream entered the lake. They had not gone far when Fingal stopped. Something was wrong.

"This is Rocky's spawning stream?" he asked, puzzled

by its taste and smell. They were vaguely familiar. Had he passed this way before?

Coral Bud saw him hesitate. "Are you all right, Fingal?" she asked. "Do you want to rest?"

"I'm all right," he answered, "but there's something wrong with that water. It doesn't taste right."

Gaffer turned back to see what was wrong. "These inland streams all have different tastes and smells. They taste of the land through which they have flowed."

"I know," said Fingal, "but that taste is not the taste of land. It's something else." A wave of nausea swept over him. Then he remembered. It was the taste that was carried to them on the tide, long, long ago, when they were in the salmon cage at the fish farm. "Farmers," he exclaimed. "Don't you remember, Gaffer, don't you remember how sick we were when farmers put pig slurry in the bay?"

Gaffer tasted the water again and this time he recognised what was wrong with it. "You're right, it's the same taste. There's something foul there. We had better keep away from it. It made us very ill when it came into our cage."

"We couldn't eat for a whole day. It was gross, much worse than this," said Bubble, remembering too.

"Eat," said Gaffer musingly. "That used to be such a magical word. I used to be so fond of food. Now, I don't suppose we have eaten for months and I don't even miss it."

"That's right," chuckled Bubble, "I remember that appetite of yours. You were voracious."

"What about Rocky and Storm?" Fingal asked urgently, "what if they've gone into that river?"

There was a shocked silence. The fish looked at each other, appalled to think of what might have happened.

Elvira was the first to voice their fears. "You don't think they've been poisoned, do you?" It was too terrible to think about.

"I'm sure they wouldn't have gone into the river if it tasted like that," said Gaffer.

"We nearly did," said Duff. "If Fingal hadn't remembered the taste, we would have swum right into it."

"But Storm and the other farm fish, they would have remembered," said Gaffer, determined to believe that they were safe.

"You and Elvira didn't remember," Duff insisted.

"What if they were already in the river when the farmer put the slurry in?" Elvira said fearfully. Gaffer wished she hadn't said that. She always managed to say the wrong thing.

The sound of many boats and the trundling noise of the approach of heavy barges gave them their answer. The lake had many boats. A few of them were used by anglers. The salmon avoided these. Most of the boats, however, were harmless. Large cruisers swept by, leaving a double line of little waves in their wake. There were speed boats which darted about, humming like gnats and sometimes tall graceful sailboats passed with creaking masts and rustling sails. The lake was where human beings came to play. However, the boats which came now brought men who came to work.

They worked fast, shouting loudly and moving about quickly in the smaller boats. From the barges they drew long lengths of floating boom which they placed in a wide semi-circle about the place where Rocky's spawning stream entered the lake. Fingal heard the throb of an engine and the churning sound of a pump in the water. It was not like the pump at the fish farm which had pumped fish into the killing tank. This pump sucked up the pig slurry which was flowing from the river into the lake. The salmon knew they should move away, out of the area, but they stayed, hoping they would discover that they were mistaken about their friends.

Two smaller boats drew away from the boom and met, just overhead. They stopped. "What's the situation up-river?" asked the man in one boat.

"Four miles of polluted water. We've traced the source. A farmer emptied his slurry spreader into the river."

I could have told them that, thought Fingal, listening intently.

"What's the fish situation?"

"Drastic. A whole run of salmon wiped out. Thirty of them, floating belly up. They're netting them out now."

"And trout?"

"Hundreds. They're still counting."

The salmon had heard all they needed to know. They moved silently away from the water near the river which was growing increasingly foul tasting and headed for the lake's deep channel where the main current flowed.

19

Spawning

They swam on blindly, not knowing where they were headed. Only the wild fish could tell which rivers were spawning grounds and which were not. Duff had been spawned in the same stream as Rocky and it was the only spawning stream he knew. Coral Bud could not be sure if it was her spawning stream or not. She had been only a young smolt when she set off downstream more than a year before. This was her first time to return to spawn. Rocky's stream had been too polluted for her to recognise whether or not it was her spawning stream too. "It's here somewhere," she said, "but I'm not certain which stream it is."

Again and again they found traces of tributary streams in the deep channel which meandered through the lake and among the islands. They waited in suspense each time as Coral Bud tasted them, but in vain. There was none of them which she recognised. Perhaps Rocky and Duff's stream was her stream too . . .

"Couldn't we choose a stream at random?" Elvira suggested.

"You can't do that," Duff explained. "A spawning stream is a very special stream, with the correct river bed. Not every river is suitable."

"If we have not found a river which Coral Bud recognises by tomorrow," said Gaffer, decisively, "then we will have to start exploring all the rivers and streams, till we find something suitable." It seemed the only sensible thing to do. They could not wander aimlessly, hoping to find a stream which might not exist.

They swam most of the night and as usual, rested for a short while before dawn. When day broke they noticed that the lake had narrowed once again. Soon, they were swimming in a strong, fast flowing river current. Occasionally they passed under old stone bridges and twice they had to leap up small weirs where the river water gushed and frothed. Trees arched over the river, shading it with green. They stopped in a dark pool. It was time to decide whether to swim on up-river or turn back and search for a spawning stream.

"Let's go on, just a little bit further," pleaded Coral Bud.

"But we're wasting time," Gaffer argued. "How much longer can we travel?"

"Do you think your spawning stream is ahead?" Fingal asked her. He had sensed, for some time, Coral Bud's intense eagerness to swim upstream. She did not seem to be fully aware of it herself.

"I don't know, I can't tell. But I know I do want to go on," she said and looked hopefully at Gaffer and the others to see if they would not agree to continue a while longer.

"It's no use," said Duff, "we must go back. It is spawning time. We must find a spawning bed soon."

"I want to go back too," said Elvira, siding with Duff.

"Perhaps we should go on a little way," said Fingal, "just a little further, till Coral Bud is convinced that her stream isn't here."

"No, I don't think that is a good idea," Gaffer insisted. "Duff is right, we must explore the streams and find a suitable place to spawn. We can't go on searching for a stream which might not even be there."

Bubble agreed. "There's no point in going any further."

Fingal and Coral Bud were outnumbered. Reluctantly, they turned and followed the others back the way they had come. "Don't worry," Fingal reassured Coral Bud, "we'll find a suitable place."

"No we won't, not this way," said Coral Bud in a distressed voice.

"What do you mean?" asked Fingal, "there are lots of streams."

"But not the right one," said Coral Bud, "I must go back." She turned with a violent sweep of her tail and swam up-river again.

"Coral Bud, come back," Fingal exclaimed and swam quickly after her. "Wait," he called, "you can't go alone."

She swam forward so fast that he could barely keep up with her. A moment later Gaffer came, speeding behind them. "Where do you two think you're going?" he shouted as he caught up with them.

Coral Bud stopped for an instant. "You can go where you like, I'm going to my spawning stream."

"Your spawning stream?" Fingal echoed in astonishment. "You knew where it was all the time?"

"Oh my," said Coral Bud, suddenly realising what she had said, "oh my goodness . . . so that's what it is."

"What is?" Elvira asked, catching up on them at last.

"I think Coral Bud has just discovered that she knows where her spawning stream is," said Duff excitedly.

"Yes, it looks that way," Gaffer agreed. "Coral Bud, you had better lead us now."

Fingal swam alongside Coral Bud as she led the way

upstream. Towards evening she chose a small tributary stream which gurgled pleasantly between wooded banks. It was a beautiful stream, with clear sparkling water and a stony river bottom.

"Yes, this is a spawning stream," Duff said, wise with the knowledge of experience. He turned to Elvira. "This will do us very well."

Elvira chose a pebbled inlet under the shade of a thorn bush which already showed the ripening red haw berries of autumn where it overhung the stream. The others swam onward and left her there with Duff.

The following morning Gaffer and Bubble found a shallow pool, protected from the rushing current by an outcrop of rocks. "We will stop here," said Bubble contentedly when she had inspected it fully.

"Couldn't we stay here too?" Fingal suggested to Coral Bud. She made no reply. With a determined swish of her tail she leapt up a small cataract and continued her journey upstream. He had no choice but to follow.

It was almost noon when she stopped at a spot where a bend in the river made a pool of still water. She nosed carefully in the gravel and looked at the larger stones on the side next to the river. "Yes," she said at last, "this is where I was born. I will make my redd here."

"Your redd?"

"A nest for our young."

Fingal looked about him at the rushy banks and the small, fast flowing stream. How different it all was to the nursery tank in the fish hatchery where he had been born. His was a pampered upbringing, free from the risks and dangers that loaded the odds against survival for wild salmon fry. Freedom for them meant living with danger every day of their lives. Yet Fingal felt envious and wondered how it would have felt to have been always a wild fish, like Coral Bud.

She was busy now, scooping a hollow in the pebbles, flicking her body sideways and lifting the stones by flapping her tail.

"Can I help?" he asked.

"No," she said firmly and went on moving pebbles till she had made a sizeable depression in the bed of the pool. Fingal circled round and round with rising excitement. Coral Bud unhurriedly inspected the nest on all sides till she was satisfied that it was just as it should be. Then she settled herself down in readiness. Fingal swam down and took up his position beside her. It was time to spawn. He quivered from head to tail. Side by side, they shed their eggs and milt on to the gravel bed.

When they finished spawning, Coral Bud moved forward and began to scoop pebbles again, moving them into the nest to cover the spawn. Fingal waited and watched. Soon, the nest was covered and a new depression made in the pebbles just ahead. Coral Bud lay in the new redd and Fingal joined her. Again, they shed their eggs and milt on the pebble bed and again Coral Bud moved forward to scoop pebbles which would cover the old redd and make a new depression which would be the next nest. Night was falling as she covered the last of the redds which she had made in the gravel bed. Their young were safe. They would stay under the cover of the pebbles till they had hatched and grown from alevins to young fry. Exhausted, Fingal and Coral Bud rested till morning.

20

The Song of the Sea

It was time to go back to the sea. As they swam downstream, swept along rapidly by the river current, they felt overwhelmed by the weariness of their long journey. It seemed a long age since they had come into the river. They were sleek, fat, shining salmon then. Now they were thin, tired kelts spent by their long journey and the effort of spawning. It would be a long, wearisome journey back to the sea.

They saw no sign of Gaffer and the others as they made their descent to the lake. They must have headed back immediately after spawning and would be miles ahead by now. Fingal found he had to stop often to rest. He no longer had the reserves of energy which had carried him on his journey upstream. Coral Bud urged him on. "Just another little bit and then we'll rest," she coaxed him. Then she too would become exhausted and they would swim on silently till they could go no further. Water lice attached themselves to their bodies and made painful wounds which did not heal. It seemed to Fingal that their journey would never end.

The days shortened and the nights grew longer. The river water was stifling, with green algae lying inches deep at the surface. The two salmon moved downstream, mechanically following the main current, heedless of their surroundings. After endless miles and days they reached the fouled stretch of dirty river which passed under the many bridges of a town.

"It's not far now," said Coral Bud, "we're more than half way."

The river widened below the town and they found themselves swimming in the lower lake. They progressed slowly, stopping more and more frequently to rest. Once they were hunted by small, ferocious mink and had to swim miles off course to escape from them. Day after day, they swam on, unthinkingly, beyond hope, beyond exhaustion. In the end, instinct alone drew them downstream.

It was late on a grey cold evening, when a red glimmer of sunset barely penetrated the stormy autumn sky, that they saw the high looming wall of the dam gleaming with lights against the gathering darkness in the sky. They felt none of the excitement they had experienced on their journey upstream. They were too tired and too sick to care.

Fingal searched the length of the dam wall till he found the entrance to the fish-pass. "This way," he called to Coral Bud. They dropped down, tumbling from pool to pool, till they reached the conduit where Fingal had been fished out on his upward journey. They swam through it and then downwards again to the tail-race below.

The tide was full. The taste of salt in the water stimulated them. "We're nearly there," cried Fingal, feeling a surge of enthusiasm for the first time since he had left the spawning stream. The salt stung the lesions that disfigured his skin but it was a wholesome feeling. He knew that the salt water would soon heal them. He looked at Coral Bud. She was wretchedly thin. An ugly sore marked her back, near her dorsal fin. Fingal felt an intense gladness that he had survived to go with her to the sea and watch her grow fat and sleek again in the rich ocean feeding grounds.

The flow of the river current and the falling tide swept them rapidly downstream, through the rocky harbour and onward to the estuary below. They heard the rhythm of surf pounding on the river bar. When they first heard it, months before, it had sung the song of the river. Now, it sang the song of the sea.

"Do you hear that," said Coral Bud ecstatically, "it's the song of the sea."

Its rhythm drew closer and closer. They swam eagerly to meet it. It thundered like a drum. Then, only a few yards away, a shining black shape shot through the water. "Look out, it's a seal," screamed Coral Bud. She turned and tried frantically to swim against the combined flow of river current and tide. The effort was futile. She was too weak.

Fingal gathered his last reserves of strength. He would face the seal. He would become its prey and that would give Coral Bud time to escape. He swam to intercept it but the seal swept by him and darted after Coral Bud. Fingal watched, horrified. Then, inexplicably, the seal halted. It circled round her. "Don't be afraid, Coral Bud," it said, nuzzling her in affectionate greeting, "I promised you I would never eat you, didn't I?"

"Is it really you?" exclaimed Coral Bud. "But you've grown enormous."

Fingal swam over, hardly daring to believe that this was the baby seal who had travelled with them long ago, on their journey in the sea.

"Gaffer was here," said the seal, "the day before yesterday."

"Gaffer? Here?" Fingal echoed delightedly.

"Yes, I met him when I was looking for breakfast."

"Oh no, you didn't eat him?" Coral Bud asked in dismay.

"Not this time, he didn't smell one bit delicious," said the seal, "and he looked worse than you do. He said to tell you that he will feed for a while just north of the estuary, so look out for him. He has some notion about going to Greenland."

"Yes, that's where our winter feeding grounds are," Coral Bud explained. "We're going there too."

"Are we?" said Fingal in astonishment. It dawned on him that this was why they had made their long wearisome journey downstream. It was why they had struggled onwards even when they were sick and exhausted. With a surge of excitement he rushed towards the pounding surf on the sandbar.

"We'll see you next year," Coral Bud called to the seal as she turned to follow Fingal down the channel, past the bar and out into the great wide ocean beyond.